She'll never forgive her attacker . . .

Seven years ago, a knife-wielding stranger left socialite Ava Camden for dead on the sidewalk of an upscale Atlanta restaurant. She survived, but her face is brutally scarred. The police, the courts and the powerful Camden family pinned the assault on only one suspect: Joel Sapphire, a twenty-year-old star athlete on the cusp of a pro football career. Too drunk to remember any details, Joel was found over Ava's body, holding the bloody weapon.

His brother is her only hope for the truth . . .

Graham Sapphire grew up fighting on the city's tough southside, and he'll never let the Camdens crush his family. Now a wealthy hotelier, he's determined to clear his brother's name—and to find the monster responsible for Ava's scars. Graham started writing to Ava the day his brother entered prison, asking her to give him a chance, and offering his help. She never answered—but she never stopped reading.

But the truth may destroy them both.

Now Joel has been paroled, only to vanish before Graham can reach him. Is he lurking in the shadows—or on the run from death threats? Ava is the lure that will bring him back, but she's not alone in the fight. Graham will give his life—and even his brother's—to protect her. The bond between them is hot, tender, and almost as dangerous as the hunter who waits in the shadows of the city's darkest streets.

All Beautiful Things

by

Nicki Salcedo

Bell Bridge Books

This is a work of fiction. Names, characters, places and incidents are either the products of the author's imagination or are used fictitiously. Any resemblance to actual persons (living or dead), events or locations is entirely coincidental.

Bell Bridge Books
PO BOX 300921
Memphis, TN 38130
Print ISBN: 978-1-61194-376-4

Bell Bridge Books is an Imprint of BelleBooks, Inc.

Printed and bound in the United States of America.

We at BelleBooks enjoy hearing from readers.
Visit our websites – www.BelleBooks.com and www.BellBridgeBooks.com.

10 9 8 7 6 5 4 3 2 1

Cover design: Debra Dixon
Interior design: Hank Smith
Photo/Art credits:
Woman (manipulated) © Stokkete | Dreamstime.com
Textures (manipulated) © Javarman | Dreamstime.com

:Lbat:01:

Dedication

In loving memory of My Father

He loved every book he read. The last kiss on his cheek was mine.

To My Mother

For being the first person to tell me I am beautiful

To My Husband

For being the last

To My Sisters

For being all the beauty in between

Prologue

Day One, Year One of Joel Sapphire's Prison Sentence

Dear Ms. Camden,

The man who attacked you should die in prison. I understand why you hate that man. I hate him, too. But I believe with all my heart that my brother, Joel, is not him. For your sake as well as Joel's, I intend to prove it. Please help me find out who really did this to you.

—Graham Sapphire

Year Three

Dear Ms. Camden,

I heard that you started a homeless shelter in downtown Atlanta. Your generosity is a gift to the city. I would be happy to assist with supplies or food if you are in need of donations.

—Graham Sapphire

Year Five

Dear Ms. Camden,

Please accept my condolences at your father's passing. I am including a check for one million dollars to the cardiac research foundation suggested in lieu of flowers. I don't think you would ever take solace in flowers.

In addition, I want to sponsor the families of out-of-town patients for the length of their treatment. As a part of your father's memorial fund, they can be guests of my hotel and will receive the same five-star treatments as our regular guests. I have asked that this gift remain anonymous. I understand if you wish to decline this offer. Regardless of my continuing belief in my brother's innocence and my on-going efforts to clear his name and find your attacker, I fully realize that you have every right to blame my brother for the stresses that contributed to your father's sudden heart attack. Again, I offer my sympathies. I continue writing these letters to you in the hope that one day you may answer.

—Graham Sapphire

Year Seven

Ava,

We received word that my brother is up for parole. I will continue to try to clear Joel's name and find your true attacker even after my brother is released. I swear on my own life that he did not hurt you. I hope you see his early release as evidence that he is, and has always been, a good person. Being drunk that night was his mistake, not his crime. Being a high-profile athlete didn't help his defense. His only desire is to resume his life quietly and to work with me to clear his name. He has only sympathy for you and hope that finding your attacker will end both your suffering. I'll never stop trying to prove his innocence, for his sake—and for yours. It's been seven years, but

Joel still gets death threats for what people believe he did to you. If he were guilty, I'd want him dead, too. But he's not, I swear to you . . .

—Graham

Chapter 1

AVA CRAWLED ONTO the child-sized bed and pulled the covers over her face, pretending the quilt was a river above her. The patchwork calmed her breathing. In, blue. Out, white. There were thirty-six squares of blue and thirty-six squares of white. Sometimes she was hidden long enough to count each one. In the distance, she heard loud whispers and stifled giggling as her nieces searched the house. She always hid in the same place, and they didn't go to her usual spot until last. They looked everywhere except where she'd be found. They enjoyed the art of seeking. But for Ava Camden, there was a joy in being hidden.

It felt silly being a grown woman in a child's bed, but her nieces expected her to dress up on command and hide so they could seek. She couldn't deny them anything, because they were like her own children. When she thought of the future, she didn't see a family. She saw a void resembling a hollow space in a tree. The rest of the world grew around her absence.

The approaching laughter allowed her little time for remorse or cynicism.

The girls climbed on the bed. This was their favorite part. When they uncovered Ava, she was hidden again in the mass of her dark hair. The long, twisted strands protected her from unwanted eyes when she needed it.

"I'm sleeping," she said. Her nieces went back to loud whispers. They put a tiara on her head and smoothed the hair away from her face. The good side was revealed. The side with the scars pressed against the pillow. She knew that when she turned to face them, these two girls would hug her and say she was beautiful.

"Smile," Lydia demanded. She was almost five and serious

and like her mother who always combed Lydia's hair into a bun like a ballerina.

Ava smiled but didn't open her eyes.

"Make a funny face," Lexi demanded. She was three. By her second birthday, she had more than enough hair to make two ponytails. It made it easier for people to tell them apart. Two years separated them, but they looked enough like twins to confuse people.

Ava puffed up her cheeks like a blowfish. Lexi's small hands popped the balloon of her face, and Ava exhaled dramatically. She felt kisses on her cheeks. No one else in the world was allowed to see her like this. If it weren't for these two girls, she would have forgotten happiness completely.

She opened her eyes to their laughter, and Lydia hovered above with a camera.

The room lit with the camera flash. It was like lightning from a distant storm. Not dangerous, but worrying.

"Let's play something else," Ava suggested. She tried not to move suddenly. She tried to keep the smile on her face even though she didn't want to. She climbed off the bed. "Can I see?" she asked as she took the camera from Lydia. She kept breathing. "Let's not play with your mother's things."

Lydia protested, "You take pictures of us all the time."

"I'm your aunt. I'm supposed to take pictures of you. Pictures are the only way I know what you look like standing still."

Lydia started to cry like she'd been punished. She asked repeatedly for the camera as she trailed after Ava to the kitchen. Her sister Nadine's house was twelve kinds of yellow, open windows, and a roof that parted rain clouds. Sunshine lived in that house.

Nadine chopped carrots with a carving knife. It was the wrong kind of knife, but Nadine didn't care. Eight chops of the knife made nine carrot pieces. She discarded the stump and tip into the trash can as she smiled. There was sunshine in her house and on her face until she saw the camera in Ava's outstretched hand. She turned down the volume of the television on the kitchen counter.

"This is yours," Ava said to her sister.

Nadine clicked through the last dozen pictures taken. She knew what Ava wanted and deleted the images. She turned back to the television and cranked up the volume again. This time it was too loud. This is how they fought. Nadine let the blaring voices of strangers be her shouting. Ava busied herself by setting the table. The girls needed juice and neon plates with matching utensils. They liked to match pink with pink, blue with blue. Ava wanted to maintain order where she could.

"Why can't we take pictures of you?" Lydia asked. She sounded like her mother, who would not voice the question other than to resume the chopping of carrots like an angry guillotine.

"You did take pictures of me," Ava said to Lydia. She tried to distract them with plain paper and crayons. They wanted no airplanes. They refused to color. "Why do you want to take pictures of me? You see me every week."

"Because we don't have any pictures of you anywhere. When you're not here, we forget what you look like," Lydia said. "And we want to see your scars. Where did you get them?" Lydia had not asked before. Both girls were born after her face was scarred. They didn't know her any other way. They didn't know what her face used to look like. There weren't any pictures of her after or before.

"I had an accident, but now I'm fine."

She said that sentence daily. In the grocery store, at the gas station, on the train.

I had an accident, but now I'm fine.

But she wasn't fine. Saying the word "accident" created another flash of distant lightning in her mind. A memory of the night her face was slashed.

Lexi stayed yellow happy like the sun. She made a blowfish face and popped it with a laugh. Lydia watched Ava with a scowl. Tomorrow was her niece's fifth birthday. There were the days of your birth and days you were unborn. Ava had both.

She wanted the girls to be different than she was. For seven years, since Joel Sapphire slashed her face outside an Atlanta restaurant, she'd been full of every kind of angry and hate. Eventually, she would need to be things she wasn't. Happy. Confident. Photographed.

And the television kept shouting at her. News headlines began to fill the room.

Baseball season was headed towards the playoffs with the Braves in position for a pennant. The Falcons had lost a third game in a row. A tropical storm brewed off the Gulf coast of Florida. It would be an unseasonably cold and rainy month here in Georgia. Local Atlanta elections were heating up.

Nadine began to dice another carrot. Ava organized the neon spoons to match the colors of the rainbow. The girls crunched carrots. Lydia refused to eat the cubes of cheese. Lexi spilled her juice. A blue cup fell to the floor.

Breaking news. Nadine stopped the angry chopping. "Ava, come see this."

> *Joel Sapphire was paroled from prison today. Sapphire, a first-round draft pick and younger brother of Atlanta businessman Graham Sapphire, served only seven years of his ten-year sentence for a brutal knife attack on Atlanta socialite Ava Camden.*
>
> *Camden, the daughter of prominent Atlanta lawyers Cecil and Sera Camden, was left with severe and permanent facial scars. The attack and trial drew national and international attention and sparked a firestorm of debate. "White man attacks black woman." Ironically, there were accusations that the Camdens' vast wealth and influence in Atlanta's black community expedited a quick verdict and sentencing against Sapphire. Camden was unable to identify Sapphire as her attacker. The Sapphire family maintains the conviction was based purely on circumstantial evidence.*

> *More controversy is sure to come as of today with his unexpected parole. Prison officials are not releasing details of his whereabouts. Both the Sapphire and Camden families have been targeted with death threats in the past. Neither can be reached for comment.*

Nadine turned off the television. Her knife hung suspended midair. No more carrots would die that day. There were eleven perfect carrot discs. Nadine put the pieces, including stumps and tips, onto a plate.

Ava closed the utensil drawer. "It means the media is at my house. Waiting. Good thing I'm not going home." Ava felt her body temperature starting to rise. More cameras. More questions. *How could he be free?* She didn't want her sister seeing her panic. "I've got to get cleaned up and go over to the shelter."

Ava walked into the bathroom and stared at her reflection in the mirror. She'd forgotten the tiara the girls had put on her head and took it off. *I am not a princess.* She pulled back her hair and examined the scars on her face. There were three long pale lines against her brown skin. Instead of being raised or flat, these scars were indented into her face. The scars ran down her cheek like dry riverbeds. No amount of makeup could cover the damage. Her hands shook, and soon her entire body trembled. Her head fell forward, and she gripped the sink in front of her. Outside, she heard wind chimes. Bells were once a musical sound, but now they were only a warning of the wind.

Memories rushed back to her. If she didn't look at herself, she didn't have to remember.

That night seven years ago, she had left the restaurant to catch a cab when she paused to look for her phone. She felt a sudden stinging blow across the back of her head. She fell to her knees and realized that something had struck her. She immediately wanted to lie down, was surprised by another hit, and twisted instinctively to see her attacker. Her mind buzzed in confusion. A shadowed form loomed over her, and Ava held up her hands to push the person away. She was struck across her face. A strong hand punched her again and again and grabbed her jaw and turned her face to the street. Her cheek scraped against the asphalt until it bled. She could see the glinting reflection of a knife in the darkness. Behind it, an eye looked down on her. It was like a mirror without color. Not blue. Not brown. It didn't blink as the knife grew closer to tear open the tender flesh above her left eye. She felt a searing pain like acid, and then her vision clouded over with red.

By the second cut across her face, her mouth filled with blood. By the third, she tried to tear at the hand on her jaw but only dragged her own blood down her neck. Three slices of the knife, and her face was carved into four unequal pieces.

Ava didn't know how long she lay there before she heard other sounds. The lazy footfalls of a person walking down the street, a scream that wasn't her own, determined running, sirens, and then whispering. Someone held her hand. One ear pressed toward hell in a pool of her own blood and a strange, deathly silence. The other ear pointed toward heaven, but all good angels were quiet that night. The bells chimed regardless of her pain.

When she awoke days later in the hospital, there had been no signs of sexual assault and later the police would console her with, "Be thankful you weren't raped." Only men would try to quantify the magnitude of pain. There was no such thing as more pain or less pain. Maybe one day her niece would prick her finger on a thorn and Ava would console her with, "Be thankful your face wasn't slashed."

Ava swallowed down the memories. Plates and glasses clinked in the kitchen. Sunshine returned. A phone rang in the other room. Lexi repeated a single verse of song. *How I wonder what you are.*

Her nieces wanted a picture of her. For them it was a simple request. Ava washed her hands and imagined holding a carving knife. She closed her eyes. She would do anything to be better for her nieces. She wanted them to be different than her, stronger than her. But they didn't understand all that was behind the scars. She was hideously disfigured, but Ava didn't need to be beautiful. She could accept the ugliness, because it wasn't the scars she hated, it was the anger. She hated the anger. That was all she saw when she saw her face.

How would Joel Sapphire react to her now? She hadn't gone to his parole hearings. She had not seen him since the trial. She was staring at herself unable to see her own face anymore and suddenly desperate to see his. Maybe it would be easier to face her attacker than look at herself in the mirror.

Ava walked into the kitchen and hugged Lydia and Lexi. She didn't mind the sticky kisses. Long after she left, their love would still be on her face.

Nadine watched her. "Please be careful at the shelter tonight, Ava."

"I'm always careful."

"No, it's Mother. She wants to see you first at her office. You know what she's going to say. Now with Joel out . . ."

"She's going to say that I don't need to work at the shelter anymore. She says it every time she sees me. "

Ava reached past the knife on the counter and picked up the camera. She handed it to her sister. Nadine, the sister, the surgeon, the wife, the mother. She used knives to heal people and dice afternoon snacks. Ava had nothing of her own to claim. He'd been drunk, then angry, now he was free. It was a terrible mantra. Ava had always believed the officials wouldn't parole him, even after she'd read Graham Sapphire's final letter.

She'd never answered Graham's notes. Not once in seven years.

"Can you take a picture of me?" Ava asked.

Nadine tucked a few of Ava's twists behind her ear and started smiling. Where there had been disapproval before turned to hopefulness. "You look—" Ava stopped her sister with a playful nudge.

"I know, I know. Don't say it."

Nadine took the camera. She didn't demand a smile and didn't get one. Ava would not look directly at her sister. The lens could steal your soul if you weren't careful. One. Two. Three. Three slices of the knife. She willed her eyes to stay open for the flash. With the flash there would be lightning. There would be the memories.

Nadine turned the display so Ava could see the picture.

"What do you think?" Nadine asked.

The first thing Ava noticed was not the scars, but the exhaustion in her own eyes. She never slept. She worked at the homeless shelter from four o'clock to midnight. After midnight she drove around the city until daybreak. When the sun came up she could sleep for a little while.

"Send the picture to me. I'll print and frame it for the girls."

Nadine arched a brow like she didn't believe her sister. If there were no pictures, there were no scars.

It would be the first picture of Ava in seven years that didn't have the caption, "Crime Victim."

Chapter 2

ENTERING THE LAW firm of Camden, Franks, & Rose discreetly required stealth and speed. Ava shook her head at the floor, her hair fell forward, and she swept it to the left. When she looked up, half of her face was hidden. She had twenty-seven minutes to get to the 44th floor and back down to her car. She had to be at the shelter by 4:01 p.m. She could be earlier but not later.

Ava registered her visit at the security desk and moved immediately toward the elevators without looking up. The guard belatedly realized who she was. He stood and offered a distant, "Good afternoon, Ms. Camden." She heard him but was far enough away to pretend she hadn't. She kept walking to get lost in the crowd. If she turned back, she'd be found.

The mass of people rushing around her smelled like soap, deodorant, perfume, and coffee. At best she smelled like carrots. All the shoes made noise, taps, and clicks, but Ava's shoes were sensible and silent. She didn't move with the speed and purpose of the other people. Down-turned face, old coat, and sideways glances were not what her parents would have envisioned for her life. She quickened her pace as she passed her father's portrait in the lobby. He watched her from the grave and from the painting.

The artist had decided to paint a young Cecil Camden for his portrait. Her father had been an athlete, tall in stature, but with the rounded features of a boy. He never seemed to age. But death would find you no matter what you looked like.

If Ava turned to the portrait, she'd see him perched at the edge of his desk, holding a pen, ready to pounce. In those days, he did things white people told him he could not do. Then later he did things that white people told him he should not do. Her grandfather had been a great success, but he stopped at the level of success deemed acceptable for a man of color in Atlanta. The family had been doctors and bankers and had enjoyed the privileges of the middle class. For her father, there was success, and then there was dominating, and then there was having no equal. And that was how she was brought up. Smarter, more serious, determined, harder working. Top of her class, law degree, place at the family law firm. Cecil didn't want to be the richest black man. He wanted to be the richest and most successful man in the city. Period. No qualifiers.

No one could have foreseen the knife and Joel Sapphire. The Camden family was untouchable in Cecil's eyes. When Ava got hurt, Joel had to pay. There was no question of guilt or innocence, only the speed of the law.

Her father had been wrong. Everyone had an equal. Everyone could be brought low.

Ava had to get away from her father's eyes. This had been her home as a child. She headed past the marble staircase flanked by Greek columns that lead up to the atrium of more muted colors and an entire floor of windows. As a kid, she had danced on the sunlight reflected onto the atrium floor. She spent her childhood thinking she'd work in this building. Ava had always lived in an ivory tower. She traded one curse of isolation for another.

Camden, Franks, & Rose was the largest law firm in Atlanta and had offices around the country, but it felt like a tomb. There were so many people moving in and out of elevators. It hardly seemed like any work could be done in all that bustle.

Ava got on the elevator and pushed the button for the 44th floor. Several people crowded in before the door closed, and a man edged too close to her. She wrapped her arms around her waist and watched the shiny mahogany floorboards. Seven planks of wood. The man continued to be too close. Ava scooted away, but the elevator gained passengers as it ascended. The brush of his shoulder next to hers made her retract into the corner.

She had no way to defend herself other than to show her face.

Ava flipped the hair back that covered the scars and turned to the man. He glanced at her and paused, because sometimes it took people a moment to register that the scars on her face weren't a strange trick of light and shadows.

Ava knew the moment he noticed the marks. She could read eyes and how they never met her own. He stifled any change in his expression and took a step back.

The beast in her growled with satisfaction. The lady in her smiled at him serenely as she exited the elevator. She would need to keep that smile on her face for her mother.

The carpeted floor of the executive level quieted the bustle. Ghosts liked quiet. Her father's purgatory in death was silence. In life, noise was as much his friend as laughter and air. He turned every moment into theater, even at home, even after her attack, even during the trial. He lured people into his gregarious affection and made them feel comfortable enough to tell their secrets. Being a good lawyer meant sifting through secrets to find the truth or enough of the truth to win.

On the night he died, Cecil Camden asked Ava to see him after her shift at the shelter. When she entered the executive level, a woman ran past crying and covering her face, but Ava thought she recognized her. Maybe she was one of the new attorneys. But this woman was different. She didn't belong. Her pixie cut hair was dyed unnaturally black. Most of the other female attorneys wore blond highlights or hair extensions. This woman wore an ill-fitting navy suit with black suede platform shoes more appropriate for dancing. Her long legs had that deathly pallor to them like she never went outside or only went out at night. She smelled like cinnamon. She was very petite but had a hunched way of walking, the way tall people walked when they tried to go unnoticed. Short people never stood that way. Everything about her was wrong. The last person you saw before your father died you never forgot.

Fewer people roamed the law firm during those late hours, but it was never completely empty. The attorneys worked every hour of the day like they were doctors in an emergency room, and affairs were treated with that same urgency. When she walked into his office, her father was alive and standing at the window looking out.

"Who was that?" Ava asked.

He called the woman "Nobody," and Ava was alarmed at the way he said that. She pressed him for what was going on. Ava guessed she was another attorney who could never live up to Cecil's standard. Like her.

"She's a liar," he said. "The world is full of liars. Like you, Ava. You aren't 'fine,' as you always tell me, are you? At any minute you are liable to break."

"I won't break," she told him. "Saying I'm fine isn't a lie. I am trying to be better," she said.

"What if I told you I made a mistake? I pushed too hard for the wrong reasons? I wanted to make the trial end as quickly as possible. I wanted us to get to the place where you could heal. And the evidence was on our side."

"Daddy, I don't understand. Is that why you called me here? Because now you regret your win-at-all-cost attitude? You never cared about me during the trial. All you wanted was a conviction. You didn't want to find out why Joel did this to me or anything. You just wanted to win. So fine. You win. And I'm fine."

He was normally gentle with Nadine and Ava, didn't speak harshly to them, but that night he had a drained look about him. Incompetent co-worker, late hour, ugly daughter who was somehow to blame for being in that restaurant, somehow encouraging Joel Sapphire to drag the Camden name into a filthy spotlight.

His anger frightened her, but she would rather have that father raging than have him gone now, forever. Even his shouting was better than his silence, sleeping in a coffin in the ground.

Ava walked past the space that used to be her father's office. Her mother had converted it by knocking down the walls and creating a casual sitting area. His ghost was there in the office, because she never felt haunted at home.

Sera Camden's office was next to that space. Ava opened the door and reminded herself to smile. Sera stood at the window and looked like a woman poised to jump to her death, except the glass prevented her.

"You should only jump if you can fly," Ava whispered.

Her mother turned with a smile. It was a Camden instinct to smile. "Darling, I didn't hear you come in. What did you say?"

"Nothing. I said, 'Hello.'"

Her mother wouldn't earn a lobby portrait until she died. Ava didn't want that kind of memorial. Once your face was on the wall, you could never hide again. Cecil had wanted to jump, and even though the glass stopped him, he found another way to die.

"You don't come see me enough, Ava. Work has had me very busy the past few months, but I always have time for you."

Instead of giving Ava a hug, her mother rushed past her to close the door and pulled a dress from a hook on the wall. It was still in the garment bag from the store. Ava turned to the window. There were three partitions and four large windows on one wall. In the distance, she could see the state capitol and the baseball stadium. Beyond that, Atlanta was covered in a vast forest of trees. There were plenty of places to hide when the sun went down or when clouds gathered. Ava checked her watch.

Twenty-one minutes remained. She'd have to leave in eight minutes to get back to her car. Her mother continued to talk about the dress.

"Before you complain, it has everything you like. It is black, but you know some color would look good on you. Long-sleeves, long skirt. It even covers your neck. You can't say you don't like it, because it is perfect. Everything you say you want. It's for the art show tomorrow."

Sera stroked the dress through the bag, but held it forward like a carcass of a hunted animal. Her mother did not like the dress, but she did want to make Ava happy. Normally, her mother bought dresses that were covered in flowers or blood red. Something was wrong.

"I love it, Mom," Ava said. This was strange. She said something and meant it. She looked up at the ceiling and expected the guillotine of Nadine's carving knife to fall across the room. "I was with Nadine and the girls longer than I planned. She said you needed to see me, and I only have five minutes."

"No, you have seven minutes. You've been calculating your exit since you walked into the door. If there was a fire in this building, how many steps would it take for us to get to the bottom exit?"

There were twenty-three stairs on each flight. There was an extra flight of stairs to get to the exterior exit below the lobby, but that was only twenty stairs. Ava stopped before the number came out of her mouth. Her mother didn't need to know those details.

"I'm not sure. A lot," she lied. "I'm trying to get to work, Mother."

Sera Camden twisted her pearl necklace around her index finger like a noose.

"I don't want you going to the shelter anymore."

Ava nodded at the words from her mother. It wasn't really words, but sounds. The usual tirade and the usual pearl twisting. Ava wasn't sure if she felt sorrier for the pearls or the finger.

She started tapping on the desk as her mother spoke, waiting for a moment of quiet. If she knew Morse code, someone somewhere might hear the distress signal and come to help. Ava learned a long time ago that if she was going to be rescued, saved, or healed, she would have to do it herself.

Suddenly her mother slammed her hand down on the desk. Ava stopped tapping. Her mother returned to twisting her pearls.

"Are you going to listen to me now?" She spoke as though the words were foreign to Ava. Each syllable slow and deliberate. "You are not going. We have people to serve the meals. You shouldn't be there."

"We don't have people to serve, Mother. I do. I have volunteers who keep the shelter running. I work with them," Ava said. "You could help, too."

"Really? I do help. I pay for the building. You want me to go down there so those filthy drug-addicted thieves can leer at me? What are you trying to prove? We used to support art exhibits and the children's hospital. This shelter cannot be the beginning and end of you. I don't think you understand what you are doing to yourself."

"I understand, but you don't. We still support the arts and the hospital. And the symphony and the botanical gardens, and you are trying to undermine the only thing I care about." Ava made a pleading step, and her mother grabbed her arm. Sera had elegant fingers, but there was one small chip in the perfect French-manicure.

"The man who slashed your face was paroled from prison today, and you still want to play Mother Teresa to a bunch of bums. I will shut that place down. I told you that I would support this outreach program, but not if your life is in jeopardy. I didn't like it before, but now it's over. You have spent your inheritance on that dump, and you refuse to go back to practicing law. Without my support you don't have enough to cover the electric bills on the warehouse let alone food, bedding, counseling. If you don't give it up, I will make you give it up."

"I never practiced law, Mother. There is nothing for me to go back to. Working at the shelter is the only work I've ever done. And I'll find the money. You don't need to be responsible for me or the shelter anymore."

Ava had been thinking of Joel Sapphire for the past hour, but this was better. The anger calmed her. Her mother was doing her a favor. She would combat anger with another kind of anger. She would replace her hatred with another kind of hatred.

"The lease will be up by the end of next month." Sera paused, and her voice dropped to a whisper. "I am protecting you. You act like nothing has happened to you. Like you weren't once lying in the street at the mercy of a man so like the ones you are determined to help right now. This job is too dangerous for you. You could get hurt. You could get killed."

"You're wrong about those men. They aren't the same as Joel Sapphire. I'm safer there than I am anywhere else in the world. Do you know what it's like walking into this building? The illustrious Camden, Franks, & Rose? This is the dangerous place. This is the place where I'll die. Like Dad. Here's what I know about the people in this building. When I was the one laying in the street, they were the ones who stepped over my body."

Ava pulled her arm free and headed out of the office. She left the dress behind.

Sera's voice rose. "You need help. This is crazy."

Ava paused. "It runs in the family. I am ugly, scarred, and angry everywhere in the world except at the shelter. You don't seem to understand. I need the shelter as much as those men do. It isn't about seeing them to make me feel better about myself. We are all the same."

She went through the door and felt her mother's angry glare at her back. If the shelter died, she would die with it. Something in her heart clenched. What was Morse code for help? Three taps, three dashes, three taps. But no one to hear the sound. She clutched her coat closer around her neck. It was cold on the streets, but it was colder in this building. Ava checked the time on her watch and started to run.

Chapter 3

THE CLOCK SHOWED 3:59 p.m. Ava held her breath until she checked it twice. 3:59 p.m. was sanity. Crazy was running through a professional building like it was on fire when the only demons chasing you were a designer dress and an oversized portrait of your father. Crazy was knowing the number of traffic lights from one end of Peachtree Road to the other end of Peachtree Street. Same road, different name. That was crazy.

Sanity was being at the night shelter before the residents were allowed in. Ava didn't like walking into a room full of people. She liked the shelter empty when she got there and then slowly filling up with people. Easier to avoid stares and easier to blend in.

She unlocked the volunteer entrance. The metal door scraped the concrete sidewalk as it opened. A group of high school students filed in to begin work. Ava checked their names off the list. She could smell the apprehension and excitement on them. They would never know hunger. They would never know fear. This was her hope.

The Light House Men's Shelter smelled like sweat, urine, and excrement. There was no amount of disinfectant that could take the stench away, and still Ava inhaled deeply. It was easier to breathe there. This was home. She put on an apron, and as she tied the apron strings behind her, she made a promise. *I will find Joel Sapphire and make him confess that he IS the one who destroyed my face, and then I will save this shelter.* She tied a knot. It was her covenant.

She would ask him why he did this to her. What had she done to deserve this kind of punishment? She would hit him until he bled. She would scream at him. She would never hide again.

She went into her office. The volunteers donated a stash of

travel soaps and shampoos. Small boxes and bottles piled on her floor. She crouched on the ground and started stacking the soaps in columns thirty boxes high. Ava wanted to stack the shampoo bottles too, but without the safe edges of a box, they couldn't be stacked without falling.

She knocked everything over. Boxes and bottles collapsed in a strange heap on the floor, and she started again. It was insanity. She tried again by making shorter stacks. Ninety-seven boxes of soap. Fifty-one bottles of shampoo.

Tomorrow she'd start hunting for Sapphire. She had people who'd track him down. What about Graham? *I can't feel sorry for Graham. He has to accept the brutal truth just like I've got to accept my scars.* Tonight she'd ignore the delivery schedule and bills to be paid. All she had to do was get through the night, and then she could fix everything in the morning.

The Atlanta fall was colder than usual. By the end of the month, the shelter would be busy, by winter it would be full. It was the worse time for her mother to shut them down. The city had plenty of freezing weather in the winter and plenty of deadly heat in summer to be dangerous, but most of the time the weather was mild enough if you could withstand the rain. For people with no place to live, rain was as bad as cold. Worse. Tarps and overpasses offered little protection from the blowing wind and waterlogged land. Everything you owned could be destroyed by rain. Tonight was probably the last dry night before the storms.

The aroma of dinner cooking was a good lure, and chili night was always successful. It was a simple meal in one bowl, warm and spicy, and complemented with a buttery piece of cornbread. Ava greeted the staff and volunteers. She kept her hair loose, covering her scars, but she didn't have to be vigilant about being covered every second. And when it was time to serve food, she joined the serving line after tying her hair back in a ponytail. She'd spend hours with her face exposed. This was the only place no one looked at her with pity.

If you put your broken face between a hungry man and food, no one noticed your scars.

AVA HAD BEEN ladling heavy scoops of chili into bowls for an hour. She hadn't eaten all day, and the chili looked inviting, but she knew that she wasn't as hungry as the gaunt men who filed in front of her. Some of them were eating their first meal in several days.

The group of students worked odd jobs around the shelter. They were from the suburbs. They knew nothing about living on the streets, being cold, or feeling hungry, but they were trying to make a difference even for one night, even if they were uncomfortable. Some of them were scared. That was all right. Being scared kept you safe. And being scared didn't make you any less good. This is why Ava loved the shelter. There were good people in the world. She needed the reminder. She'd never see this kind of goodness if she went back to work with her mother.

Ava heard her mother's voice.

Stop hiding. You are beautiful. Don't work with the homeless. Join a real law firm. Dress more feminine. Stop hiding! Wear some makeup. Go out more. Get a life. Get married. Have a baby. Stop hiding!

She wasn't hiding. At the shelter, she could be herself. The men didn't seem to notice or care about her scars, because they had seen so much worse in the world. At a big fancy law firm, even wearing makeup, they would notice her scars. The Camden family name could do a lot of things, but it couldn't end the loneliness.

At The Light House, no one stayed for long. Sometimes Ava felt sad that the people they helped passed through. Sometimes she was glad. For some, a little help was enough and moving on was the answer. It worked for Ava. She didn't like meeting people twice. The first meeting they wouldn't ask, but by second or third meeting they'd want to know about her scars. There weren't many who stayed long enough to ask what happened to her face.

I had an accident, but I'm fine.

A man paused in front of Ava. Howard was mid-sixties, clean clothes, and shaven face. He was one of the few regulars. She wanted to like him, but he resembled her father, and that similarity did not warm her to him initially. He'd been coming in for a month. As he held his tray, his hands trembled slightly. It had been much more pronounced when he first came, and Ava hoped the last bits of alcohol were finally leaving his system. Howard went job hunting every morning. Ava didn't know what he did, but she suspected he wouldn't be coming to the shelter forever.

"I'm not going back to 'Preachtree' Missions, Miss Camden. I don't know why you suggested I go. All they do is preach all day long."

"I know the people who work there. They are good people. What's wrong with a little preaching, Howard?"

"There's preaching for the word to be heard. And there's preaching for the words to be said. They are just preaching to say the words."

"I don't think so. I've heard a few great sermons at Peachtree Missions."

"'Preachtree,'" he corrected. "Miss Camden, why don't *you* preach to us?"

"I don't want to be so busy using my voice that you can't hear God's."

There were a few mumbled "That's rights," and "Amens," from the men in the crowd. *Me, a preacher?* Ava thought. *What would I know of salvation?*

"You know the rules around here. Supper, shower, shave, sleep. You need a real place to live, Howard, and those other shelters can help you with that. The Light House is temporary. In case of emergency. Those other places have a lot more services than we'll ever have."

"It doesn't feel temporary when you been here a month."

He held up his hands, and the tremors stopped. Some lost souls could be healed. But not enough. Not her.

Ava scanned the room. There were almost a hundred men bent over their dinners with rapt attention. If ever there were a safe place in the world, this was it. Tomorrow, she'd be at a fundraiser for an art gallery. She thought of wearing a formal dress and making small talk in a room full of people who felt uneasy being around her. In the shelter, she would be safe, but in the world of charity balls and social events, Ava would always be an outcast.

"Stop scowling. They're afraid to get food from you," Lance Bertram said. He nudged her with his elbow, and she released a pent-up sigh.

Lance helped run the shelter. On the night of the attack—which occurred just two blocks over, in a chic part of the city that had been gentrified by developers—he had been homeless then, wandering that nice part of the city, dodging the police and looking for a safe place to sleep. He'd seen the crowd gathering around Ava—even taking pictures of her—as she lay bleeding on the sidewalk. No one bothered to stop. The restaurant's night manager, Martin Brown, later testified that he saw Joel running from the scene of the crime.

Lance went up to them, yelling, cursing, clearing a space, then sat beside her and held her hand while they waited for the police and ambulance. Unlike the well-dressed patrons of the bars and restaurants, Lance, who had a lot to lose by calling attention to himself, didn't hesitate to get involved.

The fact that Lance stayed with her made him a sudden media hero. It made a good story. *Homeless Man Comes to Aid Of Camden Heiress.* God had given him a second chance at life, and he wasn't going to waste it. He would never admit it, but Ava knew her attack ultimately saved Lance Bertram's life.

She turned to Lance and smiled. "I'm not scowling anymore."

"Your mother lay into you again tonight?" he asked, and she nodded. "Maybe you should go home early. Make her happy this once."

"I can handle her. After our conversation, I feel like I can handle anything." She should tell him about the threat to close down the shelter. But she didn't. Lance didn't need any extra worry in his life.

"Can you handle *him*?" Lance asked and pointed to a man leaning against the wall across the room.

Ava hadn't paused since she started working, and she

continued to ladle chili as she noticed the newcomer.

The man stood with his back to the wall, both fists jammed into the pockets of his jeans. He wore a baseball cap low and over his eyes.

"Who is he?" she asked.

"Don't know. He was one of the last ones in. But he won't eat. Said he wanted to get in from the cold for a few hours. He doesn't want to stay the night either. I don't think he intends to cause any harm, so I didn't mention it to you. You like to worry over people."

"Don't you think it's strange that he stands there and looks around?" she asked. "Most people are here for the food."

He was large-framed and broad-shouldered. The layers of his dark hair were beginning to be shaggy, like he'd recently missed a haircut. The shelter offered haircuts on Tuesdays, but it was Thursday night. His beard was new growth as if he usually went clean shaven but hadn't found the opportunity to clean himself up. What little she could see of his face looked suntanned, as though he spent most of his time outside. She could make out the strong line of his nose and the fullness of his mouth. Her next thought was that he was youngish, slightly older than she. They didn't often have young white men in the shelter, and among those, never any she would call handsome, but hard times fell on everyone, women and men, young and old, rich and poor. Even the beautiful.

His clothes, jeans, and sweater, were tattered and dirty. The soles of his boots were worn down, and they were caked with red clay as if he'd been working in mud. He stood well over six feet tall. He glanced up suddenly, and his dark eyes shifted from table to table as if he were searching for someone.

As she watched him, he became aware of her stare, and his eyes met hers. His eyes were black, unlike any other shade she had seen. In her college archeology class, she had once held an obsidian stone created from ten thousand-year-old lava. Looking into his eyes was like looking into darkness so deep, even time couldn't reduce it. And his eyes also had that absorbing quality that one might associate with the night. Ava felt herself being drawn into his stare.

"Do you know him?" Lance asked.

She shook her head *No*, unable to speak. The man continued studying her with unwavering attention, and she was uncertain if she should look away or walk over to greet him. It was as if he had come to the shelter for an answer and found it in her gaze.

It was the first time since the accident that someone looked into her eyes without first staring at her scars.

Chapter 4

AVA WAS EXCELLENT at hiding. It wasn't only her hair or her hooded coat. She could disappear in a room full of people, but it was rare that someone wanted to hide from Ava.

"I should speak to him," she said to Lance as she left the serving line.

As the man saw her heading in his direction, he quickly turned and headed toward the door. What had started out as casual detachment quickly turned to apprehension. He moved with the determination of someone who ran before anyone could ask him to leave. Ava knew he would be gone into the night before she reached him.

As he got close to the door, a group of men talking blocked his path. The man tried to move right then left, but by the time he looked over his shoulder it was too late. She stood at his side.

"Excuse me," she said. The stranger kept his face toward the door. Ava did something she had never done to any of the other men at the shelter. In an effort to get his attention, she reached out and touched his back. He stiffened under her touch, and she pulled away.

"The chili is good tonight," she offered, but he didn't turn. He obviously didn't want her to see his face. She recognized that hesitation, because she often felt it herself before someone saw her face and scars. She hated that feeling of shame and felt sad that other people in the world experienced the same feeling of panic, the same instinct to hide. But why was this man hiding his face from her?

"Sir, are you okay?" she asked.

The man pulled off his cap.

"Yeah," he replied then amended, "Yes, thank you." He had good manners. Though he kept his gaze on the ground, he turned to face her. His eyes followed her retreating hand. When he spoke again, he spoke more softly. His voice was tinged with embarrassment and regret. "I'm sorry. I don't know what I'm doing here."

"The cold will do that to a person." She tried to smile but found she couldn't. "If you're hungry you should stay for dinner tonight. We had a group of high school students cooking most of the afternoon. The chili turned out quite lovely."

The man studied her with a completely blank expression. His gaze drifted over her face, down to her apron, then back up to her eyes, as if he were trying to size her up and understand her motivation.

"Lovely?" he asked. His eyes dropped back to the ground, and his voice was quiet. "What makes you think I want to eat anything described like that?"

Ava wouldn't retract her description. It would seem like an act of pity, and what she had learned best while recovering from her injuries and working with these men is that pity was misplaced on those who suffered. They didn't need pity. Neither did she.

"Everyone deserves something lovely," she said. It was something that she truly believed.

He put the hat back on his head and pulled it low over his eyes. Then he held out his hands and inspected them.

Ava's heart twisted. "No need to wash up. You're fine. Come and eat."

After a moment of hesitation, he nodded. "I guess I could eat some chili."

Ava followed him. He got dinner and picked a spot at the end of a long table. She asked if she could sit with him, and he shrugged. His magnificent eyes told her a great deal about his thoughts. Sadness, apprehension, and yet . . . relief? He ate a bowl of chili and a piece of cornbread as Ava sat across from him. He didn't lift his head much.

He ate slowly at first, then with more vigor, but his manners were impeccable. She commented on the chili, the cold night, the sweetness of the cornbread, but she never once asked him for his name or why he was at the shelter but not staying the night. Ava looked away several times, giving him some privacy, then felt his eyes on her while she spoke. He was not going to offer any clues about himself. The meal did him some good. He visibly relaxed, and she sensed that, whatever his reason for running earlier, it was gone.

"Why do you work here?" he asked. His voice was deep and graveling. He sounded like he was familiar with the streets, but he touched the napkin to his mouth and for a moment looked strangely like a gentleman finishing a prime rib dinner and a glass of good wine.

She simply said, "It's my job. It's what I love to do." If he didn't know her as the scarred socialite Ava Camden, she wouldn't introduce herself as such.

"Wouldn't it be better for you to work in a women's shelter?" he asked.

Ava remembered how she started out working in women's shelters, but many of the women lived in dangerous situations, and Ava's face, slashed and scarred, was a terrible reminder of what could happen in their lives. They liked her, but her face upset them. It wasn't history for them. It was a premonition of pain to come.

To her amazement, Ava told him that.

Why did I share that? I never tell anyone.

He looked at her face, but she bent her head at an angle so her long black hair fell across the scarred side of her face.

"What happened?" he asked so softly. His voice was tempered with a sincere inquiry. No one ever asked on first meeting her.

She looked away.

"I was in an accident," she said.

It was the lie she told people who didn't know the truth. It was easier to say that, because it was something that people could comprehend. If she told people that she had been attacked, that a man held her by her throat, beat her until she was unconscious, and sliced open her face with a knife, that story didn't get a good reaction.

"But I'm fine," she continued. "If my face and my scars make you feel uncomfortable, I'm sorry. I only came up to you so you would know that you are welcome at this shelter."

The man studied her with a slight frown. "There is nothing wrong with your face," he said.

"Nothing a mask wouldn't fix," she joked. She unconsciously put a hand on her face to cover the scars.

"That's not funny," he said. His gaze narrowed and tried to recapture her eyes, but she shifted the empty bowl between them. Their conversation stalled for a moment.

"I wasn't joking," she said softly but then changed the subject suddenly. She didn't want to talk about her face. "We have a great shelter here, and you don't have to go back into the cold. We have a few rules here, and they might make you feel more comfortable. No alcohol, drugs, sex, or fighting. This shelter is PG all the way." She pointed to a sign over the door. *We protect all who enter here.* There was another one on the outside of the building.

"Once the meal is cleared, we ask that everyone quiet down for the night. In about thirty minutes, we want all the residents to find a cot and have silent reflection time. We don't ask questions about why you're here. We don't judge. It doesn't matter to us if your wife kicked you out or the cops picked you up. You'll be safe here."

"That's quite the sales pitch," he said, observing her distracted expression.

Ava turned her eyes to the television in the corner. The sound was turned off, but the subtitles shouted at her. She felt a burning pain along the scars of her face. *Joel Sapphire released from prison today.*

She tried to refocus and turned back to the man.

"You are not the first person who needed some coaxing," she said. She didn't want to think about the news coming from the television. She didn't want to think about her attack, and she assured herself that was why it was so important to her that this man stay off the streets.

"Like I said to your friend over there," he said, nodding

toward Lance, "I only wanted to come in from the cold." He glanced around the room as he spoke.

"And another rule," she said, now intently trying to capture his gaze. "No lying."

"Really?" he asked, raising an eyebrow. "An accident, you say?" He stared directly at her face then down at the bowl with some guilt. "Sorry. Too many rules," he said.

"Too many reasons for the rules, so we keep them and make more when we need to. I didn't ask you why you were here. I was letting you know this is a good shelter if you need a place to stay for the night." There was an unmistakable reprimand in her tone, and it registered on him.

He picked up his spoon, using it as a mirror, and sighed. "Do I look familiar to you? Do you recognize me?" he asked. It seemed like it pained him to see his own reflection, as if he'd been the kind of man who used to smile a lot, laugh a lot. The spoon made a terrible mirror. She hoped it could show him the future. Maybe in another lifetime he and she would have exchanged smiles on the street, chatted over a coffee at Starbucks. Spoons only showed an inverted picture. Maybe if she saw her reflection it would be without flaw.

She shook her head, but the question made her study him closely. Dark hair and eyes. Six o'clock shadow, full lips, warm hands. A face that used to smile. "Should I recognize you?"

"I'm looking for my brother." He paused, and once again she got the sense he was hiding a lot of information. "People say we look alike. I thought he might have come here looking for a place to stay."

"I haven't seen anyone who looks like you, but you might want to ask around," she said and realized that anything else she would say would sound patronizing. An awkward silence descended over them. "I've got to get back to work. Good luck to you." She stood up, extended her hand, and waited for him to take her small palm in his large one. Again, she rarely touched strangers, particularly men, but something about him made her reach out.

He grasped her hand carefully. Even now his hand was still

cold from the night air.

"You are a very determined woman," he replied. He glanced up at her and smiled, "With very gentle hands—"

For a moment, he watched her with a greater awareness than before, and a strange notion occurred to Ava. She voiced it before she thought better of asking the question. "Should I recognize you?" She looked deep into his eyes. Nothing about him was familiar to her. His eyes weren't black as she observed from a distance, but dark, earthy brown.

Did she recognize him? She pulled her hand out of his grasp, and he let go.

He shook his head. "Not me." He adjusted the cap lower over his eyes. "I have to go, too, but I thank you for talking with me. I won't trouble you anymore, but what you do here is really . . ." he paused, "lovely."

He stood and shoved his hands back in his pockets and rocked back on his heels. His face was hidden except for his mouth. She wished he would stay. He didn't belong out there. She sensed it wouldn't be safe for him, and she was bothered that this man would go out into the cold. She was bothered that in her entire life, not only since the scars, she'd never wanted anyone to see her twice. Until now.

"I shouldn't have come here in the first place. It was a long shot that my brother would come to this shelter, but I needed to see y—" he said, trailing off as his eyes moved to the TV monitor in the corner. Ava could tell it was more than he had intended to say.

The same news story had been playing all day. She wouldn't let it affect her. *Socialite Slasher Joel Sapphire Released From Prison Today.*

"I'm sorry. Goodbye." He abruptly cleared the bowl, spoon, and a stray napkin. She appreciated the gesture, because it told her he wasn't the type of man to leave behind loose ends.

Do I look familiar to you? Do you recognize me?

She'd never seen his face before, but she knew he was lying. He wasn't sorry. He hadn't come in looking for his brother. Was he from the media? Was he trying to get an exclusive interview?

When the man left, heat from inside the shelter rushed out into the darkness. Cold air hurried in and brought the echo of a distant siren.

Whoever the stranger was, he had come here looking for her. And he'd come back looking for her again. What would happen now that she'd been found?

Chapter 5

AVA TOLD HERSELF she wasn't following the man. She was following the sound of sirens. She hated sirens because they sounded like crying. And even though she didn't want to follow the noise, she did it out of habit. Crying approached. Crying faded. The sirens could lead you anywhere. With that sound, everything in the world disappeared. The asphalt turned to water. The sea pulled her away from dry land.

She grabbed her coat and pulled the hood over her head. When she opened the door, the flashing lights became a beacon. She breathed. In, red. Out, white. He was there on the street up ahead. Head down, hands in his pockets, red Georgia clay on his boots. Is this the life his parents had envisioned for him? He didn't notice the sirens. He walked away from the sound that drew her in.

Everything was madness. Breathe in, follow the sirens. Breathe out, follow him.

Tell me who you are.

Tell me why you came here to find me.

Following him was crazy. She inspected the street and nearby buildings for something to count. Ava liked this part of the city because there was no order. Nothing could be counted because there was rarely more than one of anything, and the items she found were usually broken. There weren't enough boxes or stairs or equal things worth counting. Three cigarette butts. Two empty beer cans. A single shoe. Only someone under a spell would lose a shoe and not turn back for it.

When she looked up from the garbage on the ground, the man was gone, and she considered his disappearance a blessing. No one needed to see her twice, and the flashing lights that illuminated the streets called to her. When the world was darkest, she needed to follow the lights. She wanted to walk in the opposite direction, because the lights brought back terrible memories, but she followed the sirens as though she were in a trance. Ava reached into her coat pocket and touched her camera. She wasn't insane as long as she had something to photograph. There was too much movement in life. She had to create order and stillness.

She had once painted pictures of pine trees and the morning mist rising off Lake Lanier, the enormous reservoir an hour's drive outside Atlanta. In her other life, she was supposed to be a painter as well as an attorney. Her undergraduate advisor complained that her artwork, though technically skilled, lacked a sense of freedom and passion. Her watercolors were too idealistically perfect and her oil paintings were too bold and cheerful. Only in art was cheerful condemned. She lacked the ability to contrast light and dark. She could not reconcile reality and grit with beauty.

"Make your paintings bleed, otherwise your work will end up in a dentist's office."

The criticism from her advisor was supposed to encourage her and make her work stronger, but she wanted her art to be pretty. Why didn't people like beauty?

Ava believed that people were good. That the world was good. That things should be happy. She didn't think you had to suffer for your art.

Her advisor laughed, "Yes, you do. Look at musicians and writers."

How long ago had it been since she was so naïve? She was frustrated with art, which was never a real career option for a Camden. Going to law school was a requirement, not a choice. Even her sister Nadine was a disappointment by becoming a physician. Painting had been the only bright spot in the grayness that had been her life.

The red lights stopped moving up ahead but still lit Ava's path.

Now painting wasn't ugly enough for her. It was false pain. She needed photography. If she hid in the shadows long enough,

Ava could take pictures of real pain and blood.

Some nights it was burned homes, other nights it was bodies savaged by crime and anger. There were heart attacks and car accidents. They bled and died in the streets, but through the lens, Ava could see what the bodies were like when they were clean, whole, and alive.

You are lucky you weren't raped.

You are lucky you aren't dead.

She followed the lure of the sirens because she had to see how lucky she was. White lights, death. Red lights, alive. She rounded the corner to find blue police lights added to the pattern. Red, blood. Blue, crime. In, red. Out, blue. She breathed. She walked hidden along the trees. The sirens went quiet, but the lights beckoned.

There was a car on the side of the street. The door was open, and the vehicle was empty. A dim light illuminated the interior of the car. A body had fallen to the ground. A young woman. Shot. The wind blew, and objects clanged together. Someone's phone began chiming. Bells in the wind. It was a warning sound. A few people had gathered to see what happened. The police tried to usher them away.

She was only a few blocks from the shelter. It was hardly ever the homeless committing crimes, but other people found it a good spot to murder and rob and try to get away with it. It was, after all, a forgotten land. Nothing could be counted. No one could be caught.

Ava saw the body in the distance. She put the zoom on her camera and focused in. She snapped a picture of the body and the car. The forensic team worked to collect evidence. They hadn't covered the body yet.

A woman lay on the ground. One of her cheeks rested against the pavement as though she were sleeping. Ava took a picture. Nobody deserved to die like this. Ava took another picture and another. Anger was her breath. Anger was her blinking. She felt sorry for this woman, turning cold on the street.

Be thankful. You are lucky you aren't alive.

Maybe Ava was jealous. Better to be dead and cold than alive in hell.

Do you hear the chiming of bells? Caught between heaven and hell. The wind is rising. Do you feel the pain? Do you feel tired? Glad? Rage? Who did this to you?

The woman's car was a beaten up old thing but meticulously clean inside. An air freshener hung from the rearview window. She had wanted better for herself, and in return she got killed. There was only one wound, a single gunshot to her chest. On the ground, her purse contents fell onto the street like slashed insides.

No one should see your lipstick. Keep your wallet close to you at all times. Someone might take your money. Someone might take your life.

Ava zoomed the camera lens and focused on the entry wound. Blood dripped down her chest and surrounded her body like the sea.

Did you hear the sirens? Don't cry anymore. No one will love you, but no one will ever hurt you again.

"Ava? What are you doing here?" One of the cops broke away from the scene and walked over to her.

Ava's body tensed. Brad Vargas had been one of the first police officers on the scene of her attack years before. He shouted to the other onlookers to keep moving and go home. "You've got to stop doing this. You shouldn't be taking these pictures, and you know it. And tonight every person in the media is desperate to talk to you. My phone's been ringing off the hook all day. They are offering me big money to go on one of those national morning shows and talk about your case. Again."

He tried to grab her arm, but she stepped away from him and moved into the shadows. "Don't lay a hand on me," she warned. "You know better than that."

"You aren't afraid of the dark." Brad smiled and put his hands up in mock surrender.

"I'm not afraid of anything, anymore. And I wouldn't take pictures if your forensics team didn't work so slowly. Why is that body still in the street? Come on, Brad. Get her covered up. I'm not causing any trouble."

"You're making yourself sick, Ava. You're looking for an excuse to see crime scenes and dead bodies. What would your mother say if I told her you were here?"

"I'm not the one afraid of my mother. You are." She lowered the camera to her side and slipped it into her pocket. "And you wouldn't want to make my mother angry. Someone has to get the pictures, right?" she mumbled. Her thoughts and her feelings were crazy.

Be thankful. Who talks to the dead? The lights and sounds were too much. *Newly dead strangers. They are my best friends.*

"Does it make you feel better to see someone more hurt than you?"

"No. It doesn't make me feel good. It makes me sick. Brad, I don't have a choice. I don't want to come here. I don't want to see things like this." *I can't stop. I can't help myself. I can't say why I come.* "I want to stop."

Her hood had fallen away, and she pulled it back up. She checked the time on her watch to clear her head. Forty-seven minutes past midnight. She thought of her day. She'd been aunt, sister, daughter, volunteer. When that man entered the shelter, Ava was, for a moment, another kind of person, but she didn't have the word. Now with Brad, she was a kind of protector. She was searching the dark for predators, the same as him.

"Brad, I have other reasons for tracking you down tonight," she said. "You keep vampire hours. This is the easiest way to find you."

"What do you need?" He stepped close. Brad stopped surveying the crime scene and focused on Ava. Her scars were hidden, and his eyes were trained on the hair that hid her face like he was trying to see behind the curtain. When she played nice, he softened.

He looked at her mouth. If she told him to kiss her, he would. If she told him to take her home, he would. "I need to find Joel Sapphire."

Instantly, his mood soured. He shook his head. "Anything but that. No. I'm not the parole board. I don't know where he is any more than the next guy. I hope somebody kills the bastard."

"What about his attorney?"

"You could ask, but I doubt that drunk would remember the case or Joel."

"Drunk? I don't understand."

"Harvey Joyce dived into a bottle after the trial. Hasn't come up for air very often since. Don't you keep up with any of the gossip?"

"No. I tried to pay as little attention to details as possible—before, during, and after."

"Harvey might have received notice of Joel's parole and whereabouts. I'll ask around, but the case still causes bad feelings around the department. If anyone knows where Joel is, they might not want to say."

"Someone must know where he is. What about his sports agent? He's still young. He was a first-round draft pick. Doesn't he have a chance to start over?"

The letters. I could contact Graham, she thought. *It would be easy.* She shoved the idea aside.

"Hey," Brad said, sneering. "Give us sports fans some credit. We'll forgive and forget when players run dog-fighting rings or shoot up nightclubs, but the ladies aren't gonna let us watch a football player who served time for carving a woman's face up." He shrugged. "Besides, I doubt he's in the same shape he was at twenty."

She'd been twenty-four. A year for each hour of the day she didn't sleep.

"No more pictures. No more nights, Ava. If I find Joel, you agree to stop taking anymore pictures, okay?"

"For the kinds of pictures I take, I have to work at night. And I feel better being out at night than being at home." Ava didn't know why she admitted something like that to Brad. She was in control of the night if she didn't sleep. At dawn, she could close her eyes. "Okay. Fine. I don't want to take the pictures. I don't." That was the truth. "I'll let you get back to work."

"Stay away from here. Why don't I come by after my shift and make sure your place is secure?"

She knew what Brad was offering. He was her unofficial

bodyguard but would be more if she let him. He didn't care that he was married, but he never pressured her. He would watch over her if he saw her walking the streets at night, and the offer to care for her was always there. He was tough. He didn't pity her. He would take away her loneliness if she asked. With a gun and a badge and a uniform, he would protect her. He would keep her away from the shelter and the night. But he was another person who wanted to control her.

"Goodnight, Brad. Let me know if you find Sapphire."

"It isn't a good idea. Maybe he wants to finish what he started."

"I'm determined," she said. Before she could stop herself she remembered the tall man at the shelter. The lure of the sirens had no hold on him.

Do you recognize me?

Was he from CNN or a local new station? Maybe he was from the paper or an online tabloid. It seemed like he knew her.

There is nothing wrong with your face.

She headed back toward the shelter. There were long hours to fill before daybreak. She pulled out the camera. It was time to start erasing the past. She considered deleting images of the dead woman, but she couldn't. The more ghosts she kept with her, the better.

Chapter 6

SHE AWOKE WITH a start, her head shot up, and her hands gripped the steering wheel like her car was flying off a cliff. It was still dark in the old parking lot known as the Pigeon Pit. New parking decks had sprung up along the avenue that ran east-west through downtown, but the Pigeon Pit was a hidden gem. It was a lost catacomb the city had not figured out how to destroy. The name came from the pigeons trapped under the viaducts, but people still parked there all the same. An underground parking deck filled with pigeons. That was crazy. But it was dark and safe. Being near the university meant it wasn't unusual for a car to be parked there overnight.

She'd been wary of going home or to Nadine's, even to a hotel. Anywhere the media might be watching; these days, anyone with a camera phone qualified as a reporter. But Ava never spent the night in her car—not parked in one place, at least, which would have been dangerous. Driving all night, sure. But don't park. It was like sleeping in a snow globe. If she weren't careful, anyone could come up and smash her world. She liked to tempt fate, but she wasn't stupid. She wasn't *normally* stupid.

Don't ever do this again. Stupid and crazy don't mix.

Her watch showed 7:59 a.m. Her body was wired to the nines. She checked the time again, and the time changed to the top of the hour. She counted to one hundred and twenty, taking a breath between each number. Then she dialed the office of Harvey Joyce. 8:02 a.m. seemed like a good hour for a law firm to be open.

If Ava called her mother's work number at that exact moment, her mother would answer the phone and apologize for getting into the office late. Ava reminded herself that Sera

Camden and Harvey Joyce had nothing in common more than the BAR exam and the ability to breathe. It was wrong to hold anyone to her mother's standard. Which meant Harvey was unlikely to help Ava find Sapphire. She hung up the phone, dialed back, and left a message for the attorney anyway.

Her message was simple: her name and number. But inside her head, her voice raged.

After she left the voicemail, she dialed the number for Harvey's office again and again. She dialed all the numbers except the last digit, and she'd hang up. That was okay, she told herself. Just like sleeping in her car in an empty parking lot was normal. Dangerous, but normal. She wasn't calling him a dozen times, she was *almost* calling him. That was normal. She wasn't crazy.

I still want to kill Joel. When will that go away? I want him to die so I don't have to be angry anymore. Or afraid. Or ashamed of what I didn't tell the court at his trial. Tell me where he is. Why is he free, but I'm not?

Her phone rang, and she nearly dropped it, expecting the call to be from Harvey, but it was a message from her sister.

Birthday cake @4p. That's 3:59p for you. Then Gallery @7p. That's 6:59p for you. Craig and I will be there.

It was the day of Lydia's birth.

There was a flash of reflection as a truck drove past. Lightning, camera, sirens, reflections. Everything shone brightly when you wanted it to be dark. In the darkness, there were no memories. She was going to train herself to focus on the good memories, like the day of Lydia's birth. But that day only brought back other hospital memories of the days after the attack when Ava felt as if she'd been unborn.

Beep.

The hospital room had been cold, dark, and nearly silent. At regular intervals, a beeping sound came from the wall behind her. The pungent scent of sickness and bleach filled the air. Ava heard muted voices speaking about her face. Her slashed face. She couldn't open her eyes or talk. Had they stitched shut her eyes and mouth along with her wounds?

Beep.

Struggling against sleep, she listened intently. Two hundred and four stitches. Three long gashes from her forehead across her left eye and down her left check. She recognized her father's voice, calm and reassuring. Her mother spoke abruptly to the doctor then clasped Ava's hand in hers. Ava had never known her mother to cry, but now she was weeping.

"At least they caught him. He's in jail. He can't hurt anyone again. He was drunk. He had the knife on him and your blood. He can't remember why he attacked you. But drunk or not, he's going to pay."

Beep.

She had always been prone to bad dreams. Ava dreamed of dying. There was something worse than dying, she told herself calmly. She tried to take in a deep breath but realized a tube was in her mouth forcing air down her throat. Helping her breathe when she would have forgotten how to. Everything was imaginary from the dryness of her lips and her tearless eyes.

Beep.

She was sure her eyes were open, but the darkness was so penetrating it was a blanket covering her. It wasn't a river, but soil from her grave. She started counting then. She learned that the sirens and alarms in the hospital were the moments when she stopped breathing.

Is this what it was like to be buried alive?

Suddenly the room was filled with the scent of lilies, and the aroma calmed her, but her mother started shouting, "No visitors."

Ava heard retreating footsteps, and soon the scent of flowers was gone, too.

Beep. The bed her coffin.

Beep. The room her grave.

Beep. Beep. Beep.

The beeping continued at regular intervals all through the night and into the day. It was the only way she knew she was alive. When she opened her eyes, what terror would she find?

She did not recognize her face when she examined her image in the mirror. Her face had been covered, wrapped in a shroud for so long, she had forgotten what air felt like. In the darkness of the days before, she'd forgotten what she used to look like.

The stitches were outlined in red blood and black scabs. Patches of distortions covered her face. There were swollen places across her cheek. Blue and purple bruises marred her once flawless skin.

Ava couldn't remember if she had ever been pretty. Probably not. Her sister had always been the lovely one, but Nadine would have laughed at such a compliment, because she was smart first. If she was pretty, that was the bottom of the list. It is easy to pride yourself on brains when you had both brains and beauty.

Beauty was fleeting, and here was the proof. It was gone.

Her father was with her when the bandages came off. He carefully avoided her eyes and conversed politely about the hospital food that lay untouched before her. The unhappy vegetable broth had strangely perfect cubes of carrots floating and then drowning in the liquid.

He spoke about the weather, how well she was breathing, anything other than her face. She endured his discomfort and would have shouted him away if she weren't so tired. She hated him. He wasn't wretched or conniving, he was scared. Unable to meet her eyes.

Now that she was the beholder, she couldn't blame his gaze fixed upon the soup then some far away imperfection on the wall. Ava did hate him, but how could she blame him? He wanted perfection, and now she wasn't. This same frightening vision would greet her every day the rest of her life.

When she was finally released from the hospital, she decided that day would be her new birthday, and she treated herself to a shopping spree. For days after she got home, brown unmarked boxes of varying sizes were delivered and brought up to her room. The floor was filled with packages, but the room felt empty and echoing. Her parents made no comments about the strange deliveries. She could hear the beginning of wind. Outside her window, there was a sighing in the trees, the song of crickets, and in the distance—far distance—a siren. Somewhere, something was on fire or someone was dying. It was early evening, and after being in the brightness of the hospital for so long, Ava was suddenly in love with the night.

Ava pushed her hands through the butcher paper then tissue and tore away the covering. She turned from package to package, slid her fingers into the box crevices to open her treasures. Each one different forms of the identical gift. Soon her bedroom floor was lined with dozens of frames.

She hammered a nail into the wall and thought of the piercing of skin as her ears had been pierced as a child. She felt a momentary pleasure in ruining something, creating a small, imperfect spot on the wall. Unlike her scars, this healing would be fast. She would cover it with a reflection. Every piece of available wall space was soon protected with mirrors.

She had to see herself. She had to see the scars. She was unable to smile, both physically and emotionally, but she had to see to remind herself she was still alive.

Be thankful.

You are lucky.

Mirrors, mirrors on the wall. Who is the angriest of them all?

Ava would begin anew. She would not be defeated by despair or the impending dawn. It was the day of her rebirth. She put out the dim lamp near her bed. She would be born from light into darkness.

Ava's phone rang again, bringing her back to the present. Another message from her sister.

Don't forget Lydia's present.

Attached to the text was the picture of Ava unsmiling.

She opened the car door and walked toward the neighboring pharmacy. She could print the picture and buy a frame. She could walk slowly through the makeup aisle.

She would find Joel. She would walk into the art gallery that night. She would try to smile and make the right connections that might purchase her artwork. She needed the money for the shelter. She released her clenched fists. Too many people woke up to morning heartaches. She and Joel Sapphire were the least of all the hurting in the world, but still she wanted to make the hurting go away.

She made a list and counted the empty parking spaces she passed.

Print picture, buy frame, try on makeup. Twenty-seven empty parking spaces. Maybe it was normal to be afraid of mascara.

She stood at the entrance to the store and felt an unseen hand lift the snow globe of her life in trembling hands. How could her life in glass be shattered again if she hadn't put it back together the first time?

Chapter 7

DECATUR WAS A neighborhood just outside Atlanta with quaint boutiques, intimate restaurants, and renovated homes. Ava liked that between the bits of perfect there were still burned out, abandoned spots that no one knew how to reclaim. The town had seen its time of decay and revival. The art gallery that faced the old train depot was one of those abandoned spots. Lonely pieces of artwork on the wall, and if they were lucky, the train would pass by like the tide. It was a sound that could be both urban and rural. Creaking metal, the terrible scream of the whistle. It was different than sirens. Ava loved the sound of the train.

The front of the gallery was all glass, and the darkness of the night turned the glass into mirrors.

She took a deep breath.

Mirror, mirror on the wall. Who is the angriest of them all?

She hadn't heard from Harvey Joyce's law office. She had her required phone check-in with Brad Vargas. *No, I haven't seen Joel. Yes, I'm fine. I will try not to take any pictures tonight. No, I can't guarantee that you won't see me in the middle of the night.*

She bet her mother could find Joel Sapphire in two seconds flat, but Sera would never help her daughter with something like this. Not finding Sapphire to openly confront him. Camdens were much too sophisticated for that.

Ava looked at her watch. 6:58 p.m. She was early. Another night when she waited for midnight. She wore the dress her mother bought. Though Ava left it at the law firm, her mother couriered it to Ava's house in the morning.

There was a note attached.

People say that one day everything will be better. But they never say which day. I hope today is that day. Sometimes you forget how strong and beautiful you are.

Love, Mom

No apology for closing the shelter or putting a hundred men on the street. But her mother offered a different type of kindness. Beautiful dresses and constantly trying to create normalcy. Sera often set up dates for Ava with Atlanta's most eligible men. Lawyers mostly, then some in business, a few academics, and when desperate, a doctor or two. Tonight was not as bad as a blind date orchestrated by her mother, so Ava decided to wear the dress and do all the things her mother had been asking her to do for years. She put on a little lipstick and mascara. No other makeup. Blush or foundation would only draw the attention to the marks on her face. Better to leave it natural.

Sera knew her daughter wouldn't wear anything short or revealing too much cleavage, but this was another kind of alluring. When she pulled on the dress, she was surprised. It was long and black and seemingly plain until the material slid over her body. The cashmere-like sweater dress clung to her body, the side slits completely invisible until she walked. Ava wore a simple pair of heels. Her feet clicked and tapped as she walked, and she missed her usual silence.

Against all the black, she wore a long pearl necklace. It had been her grandmother's. When Ava was nervous and no one could see her, she liked to put a single pearl in her mouth and run the roughness of it across her teeth and tongue. One hundred and two white pearls. She had a different prayer for each one.

Please God, don't let anyone look at me.

Please God, don't let anyone talk to me.

Maybe those were wishes, but anything that started with "Please God," should be a prayer. She arranged her hair and made sure it covered half her face. Not much choice with hairstyles. She wore it down. As long as she was hidden she was safe.

Everywhere in the room Ava heard the ringing sound of china and glass accidentally touching. Whispering voices mingled and rose, echoing in the high ceilings of the art gallery.

She was relieved to hear her mother laughing in the distance. Ava knew the best way so soothe Sera Camden's disappointment was to do something respectable. The art show was respectable, and her mother enjoyed socializing with the elite art crowd. Sera felt proud of her daughter's photography despite the edgy subjects. It made the wealthy feel compassionate to see the poor and disenfranchised without having to get too close. Ava knew the only reason her artwork was on display was because her last name was Camden.

Ava had three series on exhibit. The "Less Traveled By" photos were images of Atlanta streets devoid of people and cars.

The second series was called "Ashes." Ava had photographed buildings and homes reduced by fire, either arson or accidental. Though the thought of fire frightened her, she loved burned places. Her favorite picture was that of the front door of a house. The frame remained, but the walls were gone, destroyed by heat. She loved how exposed the house looked. It could hold no more secrets.

The last series, "Faceless" started when she was released from the hospital and met Lance Bertram. He had gone into hiding after all the media attention, and when Ava finally found him she wanted to take his picture as a way to remember and say thanks. After she developed the picture, his eyes, like hers, seemed dead. Lance got into a treatment program, and eventually he and Ava worked together to start The Light House Shelter. He would never feel comfortable too far away from the streets. He stayed close by, helping other men like him—men who needed little things—sometimes food, sometimes a handshake, and sometimes a place to rest their heads for the night.

She photographed the nameless and faceless so people wouldn't forget that everything in their lives was a blessing, a gift. Her family had wealth, influence, and everything in excess except friends. There were the people her family socialized with, but when she got attacked, no one she knew understood what she went through or how to react to her. All she had was her abandoned law degree, the men's shelter, and her camera. She'd sold a few photos over the years and given the money to the shelter. It would never be enough money to keep the shelter open.

Make your paintings bleed.

All of her photos were in black and white. Besides Brad Vargas, no one knew about the crime scene photos. *There* was the blood. *There* was the pain. Her art advisor had been wrong, people only wanted to see pretty things.

Ava and two other artists had their work on display. They had several showings throughout the year. It was a black-tie affair, and her mother thought it was good for her to be out and dressed up. Ava spoke to a few people quickly but mostly kept to herself. As she moved through the crowd, she stayed to the periphery, and her scars faced the wall.

Ava scanned the crowd and, for a moment, thought she saw a tall, somehow familiar form across the room. She could make out wavy black hair and a strong profile, but as the crowd shifted, she lost her view. When the crowd parted again, he was gone. Another apparition; she had been thinking about the man she met at the shelter all day.

A million explanations raced through her head. She felt sure he did not really have a brother. Ava looked at the hand he had touched and squeezed it into a fist. If he was from the media, he'd have her mother to contend with. No one got too close to a Camden without first going through Sera.

She felt a hand on her shoulder and jumped. She was surprised to see Nadine there so early, and her husband, Craig. Nadine wore a short red dress and her hair pulled back in a high ponytail, but with the hair loose on top. Normally Nadine's hair was secured in a bun, but she let the curly ringlets spring out of the ponytail like bolts of dark lightning.

Neither of the sisters wore it straight anymore. That had

been the fashion when they were young and brave enough to waste hours with a blow dryer and flat iron. In order to be accepted in their mostly white private school, they had to wear their hair like the other girls. It was after the accident that Ava went back to her natural roots. First she had cut off all her hair in anger, and then she realized the haircut was a good thing. Being afraid was a good thing. It kept you safe. Being angry was a good thing. It made you change.

Ava wasn't brave enough to keep her hair short for long. Once it grew back, she kept it in long, twisted extensions that went past her shoulders.

Rapunzel, Rapunzel, let down your hair.

Nadine gave Ava a quick hug and kiss on her unscarred cheek. Ava felt the stickiness of her sister's lipstick on her face. She would have called the stickiness of lipstick love on her face, but then she noticed that Nadine was frowning.

"You didn't come by for Lydia's birthday cake," Nadine said. "Now you are oh-and-five."

"Please, Nadine. I was with you yesterday."

Her brother-in-law leaned in and kissed Ava, too. "It's okay, Ava. But we did miss you."

He shifted his bow tie. He was a science guy through and through. The world of Camden social events was as much torture to him as Ava. When Nadine wanted to marry Craig, their father objected, but then Ava's attack occurred, and their dad couldn't deny his undamaged daughter anything. So many people's lives were saved when she got her scars. A curse and blessing.

"No, it is not okay," Nadine said. "Five birthday parties and five no-shows. Ava said she would be there. If she isn't going to show up, she should say, 'I'm not coming.' That is okay. Honesty is okay. I'm here at an art gallery on Lydia's birthday to support her. But she wouldn't do the same for us."

"I wanted to come."

"One day you are going to have to start doing all the things you say you want to do."

Ava took a deep breath and scanned the room. She guessed

there were three hundred people milling about, and exactly three of them wore red dresses. Most were in black like Ava; it was her camouflage. One hundred and fifty black dresses. One hundred and fifty black tuxedos. Three red dresses. She breathed in again. In, black, lost. Out, red, found.

"Nadine, you said come over at four o'clock. You said birthday cake, but you didn't say how many people would be there. How many kids were there? How many other adults?"

Nadine grew quiet.

"I wanted to be there, but I'm not ready. What if those kids started crying or asking questions about me? Look, Nadine. I am trying. I thought I could go to your house, but today was Lydia's party plus this art event. It's too much for me. I can't even stand being here, but I have to be here. And I'm wearing this stupid dress that mother bought for me. Look at me. I'm shaking. I'm wearing mascara for the first time in seven years. I feel like I'm going to scream."

Craig took a cautious step back.

Nadine laughed.

"You're wearing mascara for Mom?"

Ava nodded.

"Your eyes look amazing. And the dress. Mom bought that? Okay, confession." Nadine paused. "She's trying to set you up again."

Ava shook her head.

Nadine nodded. "He's six-foot-five and, get this, an artist," Nadine said as she pointed into the crowd.

Ava looked through the mass of people and spotted a tall blond man with shoulder-length dreadlocks. He was taller than everyone in the room and not in a tuxedo. He wore a poet shirt with a few buttons open. From the waist down, he was a man out of time. He wore a kilt.

"That's Adonis?" Ava asked.

"Actually, his name is Apollo. His hair says Rastafarian. His outfit says Highlander, but his parents named him after a Greek God," Craig offered. "Should be interesting."

Ava smiled slowly. "Craig, you're in on this, too? I

trusted you."

"I'm not crossing your mother. No man is perfect, but this guy is as close as you can get."

Ava took a sip of her water and glanced at the Goliath. She never really went for that blond-haired, blue-eyed Viking type, but she had to admit the man was attractive.

"Mom is desperate. He is white and an artist," Nadine teased. She pointed at one of her fingers and continued to count each finger on her hand as she spoke. "Let's see. Mom's tried to set you up with every black single lawyer in Atlanta. Then she found a handful of Latino attorneys to parade in front of you. Two Asian MBAs."

Ava interrupted, "One was a JD and MBA. The other was GQ gorgeous, way too stylish, and a hip-hop enthusiast."

"Then there was the Indian guy who was a chemistry professor."

Ava smiled thinly, "Yes, the academia years. Chemistry professor. He had a great sense of humor."

"And now the artist," Nadine said.

"If you liked the chemistry professor, then why this new one?" Craig asked.

"Mother is a great connection to have in this city. She says, 'Take my daughter out, scars and all. Make sure you tell her to come back to work for me.' Guess, what? Men will take you out when your mother can get them a partnership or a promotion. I have to say that the Viking is a little different."

"Good different?" Nadine asked. She didn't smile, but Ava knew that hopeful expression when she saw it on her sister's face. She'd seen it when she handed Nadine the camera the day before and asked to have her picture taken.

"Not good different. In the end, he'll be the same. I don't want to date anyone. I don't want to sit across from another man who either avoids or fixates on my scars. Some people live happily single. Mom thinks of it as being alone, but I don't. I'm not alone, I'm single. 'Alone' means I'm looking. 'Single' means I'm complete. I would have been this way with or without the scars."

It was then that she noticed that the Viking spoke to another man. They were about the same height, but the dark-haired man was familiar to her. She tried to think of why she would recognize him. Then the crowd shifted again.

"I'm guessing you don't want an introduction?" Nadine asked.

"No." Ava took a sip of water. Her hands shook as she placed the empty glass on a nearby table. A waiter passed, carrying an hors d'oeuvres tray. Ava picked up a pastry and popped it into her mouth without looking at it. She wondered about the person she glimpsed near the Viking.

Nadine glanced from Ava's concerned expression to the crowd that ebbed and flowed around them like the tide. "Ava, you don't look all right. Let's try to find a seat somewhere." Nadine led her through the crowd. Her brother-in-law chatted along the way.

Craig was a doctor like her sister, even trying to heal people with his words and distract them from their troubles. Nadine was a surgeon. She had her knife, and Craig was an oncologist. Sometimes he healed people by filling their bodies with poison. Healing hurt. She avoided it.

"Have you heard about that new boutique hotel in Buckhead?" Craig asked as he continued to make small talk. "It's called the Donovan. I met the owner earlier tonight. He was studying your photographs. It might be a good connection to make."

Ava had not heard about the Donovan Hotel, but no doubt her mother had. Sera knew about every new investment-related project across the city, good or bad. Good meant investment. Bad meant lawsuits.

"There he is," Craig pointed out.

There was the man again. He stood across the room with his back to her. His dark hair was longer in the front than most other men wore it, and he ran his hands through it as he stared at one of her photographs on the wall. She couldn't think of why she thought she knew him. The only people Ava knew were from the shelter.

She paused. And stared at his back.

The only people she might casually recognize were regular volunteers or residents at the shelter. Residents like ones who needed to come in from the cold but didn't want to stay the night.

Chapter 8

AT THE MOMENT when he started to turn, Ava tensed. She wanted to see his face, but suddenly she didn't want to be seen. Maybe her exhaustion was playing tricks on her. She tried to spin around quickly, but their eyes met as she turned away.

Those dark obsidian eyes met hers.

He seemed as surprised as she felt. His eyes didn't stray to the shadowed side of her face. She wanted him to notice her scars, because then he would go away. Why couldn't he see them? They were her only shield from the world.

He was clean shaven and in a perfectly tailored tuxedo down to the silver cufflinks. She'd called him handsome at the shelter. Downturned face, imposing height, but now he was beautiful. Elegance and lies. He wasn't homeless. He wasn't a reporter. The event was for patrons of the museum. Exclusive patrons with enough money to make a donation worthy of a hospital wing or university library.

Her brother-in-law nodded his head towards Ava's art photography.

"He was taking notes on your photographs. He said he liked your nature pictures, you know, the empty roads and tree-covered paths. Maybe you could negotiate a deal with him and make money for the shelter that way."

She already put every cent she got back into the shelter. It would never be enough. Nadine said nothing, because on the issue of the shelter she sided with her mother. She'd rather see the shelter close down than see Ava go there night after night.

Before Ava could stop him, Craig guided her toward the man.

"Mr. Donovan?" Her brother-in-law asked.

"Dr. Wesley. Nice to see you again."

Nadine's eyes sharpened on him like a knife. Then it was gone. Did she recognize him? She still accepted his hand when her husband introduced them.

"This is my wife. Dr. Nadine Camden. And this is my sister-in-law, Ava Camden. You were just looking at her art work."

He was staring at Ava's eyes. He extended his hand, and only when she accepted his touch did he say, "Your artwork is lovely. It's like you have this planet all to yourself."

The careful slowness of his words surprised Ava. Men were usually excessively exuberant around her. They tried to let their happiness and loud voices cover up her scars.

"Thank you," Ava said. Their joined hands had not yet parted. His hands were no longer cold. He pulled away and opened his mouth to say something more but closed it without uttering another word.

Do something to make me hate you. The casual arrogance that he showed her brother-in-law disappeared when he turned to her. Ava hated herself for the feeling, but she was happy to see him. Then confused. Then resentful. They both wanted to run away from each other. Why had he been at the shelter?

"We were going to find a seat," Nadine interjected, trying to pull Ava away. She scowled at the man the way Lydia did when she was punished. Nadine always sensed Ava's discomfort around men.

"Are you twins?" He asked, turning to Nadine.

Ava held her breath. As children, they were as alike as Lydia and Lexi, and their mother had the habit of dressing Nadine and Ava in identical outfits.

Some of the venom in Nadine's eyes died. She reached out and squeezed Ava's hand.

"We always used to pretend we were twins."

He smiled at her then to Ava. "Do you mind if I ask you about your artwork?" He nodded in the direction of the exhibit.

They stepped out of the crowd and into the quiet space of the photos.

"Ava . . ." he began.

She kept her eyes on the wall and observed the unpredictable pattern of the photos on the wall. Three grouped together. Then four. Then one picture alone. She wanted to count them. But with his presence next to her, she could not find any order in the design. They stopped in front of her least favorite photo. It was the sun coming up over the lake in Piedmont Park. Though the picture looked empty, the park was full of runners at five o'clock in the morning. Often when she thought she had found an isolated spot, it turned out that she was seldom alone.

"Very nice to meet you," she said tightly. "Again."

"I apologize."

He studied her intently. What was he looking for? Would she know when he found it?

"Maybe you should explain what's going on here. Mr. Donovan, is it?"

"Yes. I mean, no."

"Still in disguise?"

She moved to tuck the hair away from her face so he could see her scars, the way she did every time she felt cornered.

"Don't do it. Please. Don't shut me out. I'm not afraid of your scars. They don't shock or offend me."

Eyes that wavered between black and deep brown captured hers in his steady gaze. The same elusive deep voice that had haunted her since the night before now addressed her with polish and calm. "I'm sorry," he said firmly. "I'm making you uncomfortable. I don't mean to."

Ava knew the incidental betrayals of life. She had been attacked, had her faced slashed, and had to live through the difficult and sometimes seemingly hopeless process of recovering. The shock was often too much to bear. Then her father died, and that was another betrayal, the kind that came from living life, but still paralyzing. There were smaller kinds of betrayal that the innocent suffered, and that was trusting people.

"I'm sure you have a good reason for masquerading as a homeless man and showing up here to surprise me. But I don't enjoy being *stalked.* We don't have anything to discuss." She turned away, but he stopped her with a sentence.

"Please. I need your help."

She turned back. "Why?"

"I wasn't lying about my brother. I was and I am still trying to find him."

"Is that really the truth?" she asked. "Is he homeless?" Her hair fell away from her face and cascaded across her shoulder. For a moment she forgot about her scars. "Like you?"

"I didn't say I was homeless. You assumed I was," he said softly.

"So that makes it better? I spent the day worrying about you—" she broke off.

His expression changed. His eyes grew dark and questioning. "Would you have spoken to me if I told you I was rich? Or would you have sent me away?"

She turned her head, and her hair veiled her face again. "I don't know what I would have done, but you didn't have to lie."

"Neither did you," he said. His voice was so quiet she wasn't sure she heard him correctly. Ava opened her mouth to respond, but nothing came out. He stepped closer to her but was careful to keep his distance. "I know how you got your scars," he said gruffly, "and it was no accident." His scent was citrus and pine. He smelled a little like the trees that guarded her dreams at night. "I was at the shelter because of my brother and because of *you*. I thought he might have gone there because he knows you."

"Why would he know me?" Ava asked. She shook her head. His eyes and his scent were confusing her.

When he spoke, his voice was quieter. There were no bells or sirens or flashes of light. Quiet was another kind of warning. "My real name is Graham Sapphire. You do know my brother. Joel."

Chapter 9

AVA DID SOMETHING he never expected. She clenched her fists and smiled at him. She did not strike him, and she did not immediately say a word. The warm art gallery had taken a sudden chill with the musical sound of her laughter. The guests continued their conversations in the distance, and a few turned to glance at Ava and Graham.

"You aren't worthy of my anger. You aren't worthy of anything from me except my pity. And I pity no one." She took a step closer to him.

"You have every right to be angry," he said quietly. Without taking a step back, he turned his face, exposing his cheek. "Hit me if it will make you feel better."

"Look at me."

He did. She stared up into Graham's eyes, her gaze an intense challenge. She was a fighter. Graham felt the same sharp awareness he had felt the first moment he had seen her, deep in thought as she worked behind the cafeteria line at the shelter. She was a beautiful woman with an expression both guarded and welcoming. The first thing Graham noticed about her was the wildness of the hair that fell in twisted locks halfway down her back. She tended to try to hide behind it, allowing the long hair to fall across her face as a defense mechanism.

He appreciated all beautiful things. As she stood before him poised, scrutinizing every inch of his face, and liable to strike him, he thought she was the most incredible thing he had seen in his life. She didn't step away from fear, she walked up to it.

She gave him a chilling smile. "Get away from me."

"I'll leave," he said, backing away when she didn't hit him.

Ava started shaking her head. It was more than a rejection. It was as though she was trying to silence the voices in her head.

He was surprised by the urge he felt to pull her into his arms to calm her erratic movements.

"If I told you who I was yesterday," he said, "it would have given you twenty-four more hours to hate me. We'd have had no chance of making a connection at all."

"You are right. I do hate you. And if I ever see your brother again, I will kill him with my own hands," Ava said. Her voice rose, and her head shook from side to side.

Nadine appeared by Ava's side. "Is everything all right?" she asked.

Ava continued to shake her head. She closed her eyes without speaking.

"What have you done?" Nadine asked with panic in her voice, but this time she turned to Graham.

He paused, unsure of how to explain himself, but Ava whispered as though she were in a trance, "It is Joel Sapphire's brother."

Graham bristled at being referred to as *it*.

Nadine stepped back from Graham and stared at Ava. "That's why I knew you. From the trial. So Graham Sapphire is masquerading under a different name for this venture into hotel investing?"

"Donovan was my mother's family name. It's not a secret."

"The Sapphire name is certainly not one you'd want to advertise in the hospitality business; I suppose that's understandable." She swiveled toward Ava. "I'll get Mother and call the car to pick you up." She turned back to Graham with a simple order. "Stay away from her. We have security people who will intervene if they have to. Ava? Ava, try to calm down. Are you listening?"

Ava opened her eyes. Her breath shattered on each gulp for air.

"Need your inhaler?" Nadine asked.

Ava shook her head.

"Relax. Do you remember why butterflies flutter their wings?" Nadine clasped Ava's hands. Graham had no idea what the question meant, but it seemed to soothe Ava. She straightened her shoulders. Her breathing returned to normal, and she turned away from him.

Ava walked toward the maze of photos in the exhibit hall, her movements stilted and controlled like an automaton. It was as if he ceased to exist. He apologized to Nadine, who blocked his way. There was enough sorrow in his heart to bring him to his knees.

"We don't need your apologies, Mr. Sapphire. Unless you can apologize for all the people over the years who said she deserved the attack. Can you apologize for the people who thought our family should die? How dare you come to us expecting any kind of sympathy."

Graham could still see Ava heading further away from him. "Nadine, you are right. This was a mistake, and I will go." He paused and added. "If I could apologize for every person who has hurt your family, I would."

He forced himself to remember that he was doing this for Joel, who had walked out of prison and vanished. Joel had grown increasingly despondent over the years. Even to the point he suggested it wasn't safe for Graham or their mother to visit. Now that Joel was out, Graham had a small army of investigators searching for him. But Joel had one amazing talent aside from his ability on a football field—an uncanny ability to hide. It was something his brother had in common with Ava.

How many times had Graham taken punches for him? Been expelled from school? Carried Joel home when he had skinned his knee too badly to walk? Graham had even given up his own food so his brother could eat when they didn't have enough to go around. He had made sacrifices to care for his mother and his brother, Joel.

When the guilty verdict was read against Joel, cheers had erupted in the courtroom, along with a rush as reporters ran for the doors. In the commotion, Graham reached across the partition and pulled Joel into a clumsy embrace for one quick hug before an officer shoved him away. It hurt him that his brother had lost so much weight. The gravity of the trial had taken its toll on Joel—on everyone. Graham watched his brother, shackled and diminished, be taken to prison. Graham was certain of a few things: Joel was innocent, and Ava was the key to proving that. But she was also the last person on earth he wanted to hurt in the process.

He'd learned early that taking a stand meant taking a risk. When he was nine years old, his father had knocked him down twice for defending his mother. His father dared him to get up a third time, and Graham did. He thought another beating was the worst thing that could happen to him, but he hadn't imagined that his father could think of and do worse. He had the scar on his side to prove it.

Writing to Ava all these years had been a risk. Walking into The Light House had been a risk. How could he expect her to help him? This Ava was not the one he'd met at the shelter; the woman who sat before him as he ate chili. She'd watched him with curiosity and kindness.

The men nodded at her with a bit of reverence they didn't show the other volunteers. Ava Camden was a stunning portrait of elegance, despite her baggy cargo pants and oversized shirt. When her hair fell over her face, she was trying to protect her scars from unwanted stares, and it had the opposite effect on Graham. He found it difficult to look away from the delicate half of her face and the mysterious, sad smile.

Graham remembered how his breathing slowed as she spoke, the food developed more flavor, and his worry for his brother disappeared for those brief moments. The only other time he felt that calm was when he worked with his foundation to build houses for families who were in need. The other donors gave money, but Graham liked to see a pile of wood become a home. He'd helped build in Atlanta and overseas, and he guessed both he and Ava were in the business of sheltering people from the storm.

Graham watched Ava until she disappeared. What would she say if she knew that she wasn't the only one who hated Joel? Sometimes Graham hated his brother as much as he loved him.

Chapter 10

AVA TRIED TO bring herself back to the present. She reminded herself that she was safe in an art gallery, and no one would ever hurt her again. She coughed and covered her face with her hands.

Sera Camden was suddenly in Ava's path.

"Ava, what happened? You're in a trance," her mother said as she rushed forward. She pulled Ava's hands away from her face.

"I'm fine, really."

I had an accident, but now I'm fine.

"You're ice cold and shaking. You have to stop doing this to yourself," Sera ordered.

"What did *I* do? I showed up, perfumed, and am as pretty as I can get. I have made smart conversation. I've even smiled and tried to be happy. Isn't that what you wanted?"

"I didn't come in here to argue with you. Please tell me what upset you." Despite their differences, Ava knew her mother would do anything to protect her.

"Graham Sapphire," Ava said. "Joel's brother. Here. I spoke with him." She wouldn't mention that she had spoken to Graham last night at the shelter. It would mean her mother would shut the shelter down immediately. Ava also didn't mention the letters Graham had written her over the past seven years. She'd written a response to every letter and then put her response in an envelope, never to be mailed.

Sera's face changed from motherly concern to cold anger.

"I will contact security here first, and then I'll call the police." She glanced at her watch. "We can get a restraining order by tomorrow morning. We warned the parole board about Joel Sapphire, but they opted to keep him under minimum security anyway. Now he has been paroled, and his brother is stalking you—"

"Mother, please slow down. No one is stalking me. He is a legitimate guest, and he says his brother has disappeared. I honestly believe Graham Sapphire is a decent human being who's caught up in this miserable situation through no fault of his own." Ava didn't know why she was defending the man who had so recently rattled her nerves, but if her mother had her way, Graham would be dealt with too harshly. It was discreetly known that Father had used their influence to undermine Sapphire business interests in Atlanta, which was probably what had driven Graham to use his mother's name in the hotel venture. "Anyway, it's already over. He probably already left. Nadine called the car so I can go home."

"Go," her mother said.

Sera headed over to the gallery owner in hopes of finding out more about Graham's attendance that night. In a few moments, Ava's mother would know a lot about Graham's interest in her daughter, and by morning she would know everything.

Ava had spent most of the trial not looking at Joel, and it was no wonder she didn't recognize his brother. Ava didn't want to remember anyone's face, from the bailiffs to the reporters, the judge, jurors, guards, no one's. Her face had been on display. Hers. She had not been accorded any privacy, any dignity, at all. They would never forget her face. But she did not have to remember theirs.

Nothing compared to the agony she'd felt as she waited for the jury to return with the verdict. She remembered sitting in the back of the courtroom. Her hair fell in a dark curtain over her face, particularly obscuring the left cheek and eye from view. Even though it had been a year since the attack, the wounds hurt. She'd closed her eyes and felt pain shooting across her cheek, as if her face was tearing apart.

The stitches were gone, but she could still count them in her mind. Other days, she didn't want to know the number of stitches. While she recovered, she'd go into dark stairwells of the

Camden, Franks, & Rose building, counting as she climbed. The exercise made the pain go away for a little while. She hated the itching as her scars healed. During the trial, she hated something more, waiting. She wanted everything to be over, sometimes her life, but most for her attacker to be sent to jail for a very long time.

She remembered reading about phantom limb syndrome, the presence of a pain or itch in an appendage that was removed, amputated, gone forever. She hadn't lost a leg or an arm, but something was missing. Something was stolen from her that could never be replaced.

Ava lost some of her sanity, her ability to have a trusting and intimate relationship with a man, her faith in a happy future, and the deep well of hope in her soul. Her soul was fading. She was disappearing, becoming a phantom.

Ava had closed her eyes against the sight of the twelve jurors entering the court room. She knew they would not look at her. She had evolved into the invisible. People afraid of staring at her scars didn't bother to look at her anymore.

She was disappearing. Her mind, her soul, her face. She could only think of her face as another type of phantom, gone and present, damaged past repair.

The pain in her face dissipated as she watched the final person take a seat in the jury box. Seven women and five men.

In the courtroom, murmurs turned to whispers then silence. The judge entered, and Ava regarded the judicial robe as something pretty. Long, black, silky fabric. Something you could hide behind forever.

"Have you reached a verdict?" The judge asked.

"Yes, we have, your honor," the forewoman said.

"Please state the verdict."

"We the jury find the defendant—" she paused as her voice unexpectedly went dry, then cleared her throat "—Joel Matthew Sapphire—guilty of aggravated assault."

He had nearly killed Ava and left her for dead. If Martin Brown, the night manager, hadn't run up, he might have finished the job. A new wave of anger rose in Ava's chest. Where was the feeling of relief she was hoping for? What happened to justice satisfying her rage?

Her parents sat on either side of her, but she wished her sister was closer by. Nadine held her pregnant belly with one hand and her husband's hand with the other.

A few stifled sobs went up as Joel turned to his family. He was huge, muscled, a star football player, and yet he had the bewildered expression of a lost child. His tall older brother stood suddenly, shoving his way past the outstretched arms of the guards to embrace Joel. Ava had only ever seen Graham from behind. She remembered how he held his brother. They were all fragile.

We are all made of glass. Snow floats around us. We are delicately made, meant to be smashed.

Except her father. He was the one who looked triumphant. Nobody hurt a Camden and got away with it.

Now Ava wondered if she would have thought Graham Sapphire handsome if she'd gotten a better look at him five years ago. That thought, unbidden, made her furious with herself. And yet she stood at the coat check in the art gallery and scanned the crowd for him. She saw him leaving. Like the night before at the shelter, he had no coat. Maybe he wasn't afraid of the cold.

There was an indefinable roughness to his mannerisms. She recognized that feigned aloof indifference. Hadn't she also mastered giving the impression that she would rather be alone than excluded? Graham and his brothers were raised in poverty, and the tabloids had called them "poor white trash who made good." Ava cringed at the description. She could accept criticizing Joel for his crime but not his social status.

She had never wanted for anything. Her family was wealthy. What she needed, her parents gave her, and what she wanted, they taught her to work for. When Graham glanced at the art gallery crowd as though he wanted to be an outsider, Ava recognized the insecurity in his face and the hard exterior he built to protect himself. It was something she had come to know well in the years since the attack.

He shoved his hands in his pockets. Ava stiffened as she

noticed two security officers heading his way. To her relief, he strode out of the gallery before they could reach him.

She coughed. Her throat felt dry and itchy, and her lungs fluttered with an asthma warning brought on by stress; in the back of her mind she dissected the pastry she'd eaten and wondered if one of her food allergies had kicked in as well. She would deal with an allergy attack if she had to.

Unlike the last time he left her, this time Ava wasn't worried about Graham Sapphire's safety or distracted by the sirens in the night.

She grabbed her coat and followed him into the cold.

Chapter 11

A LIGHT WIND fluttered down Ponce De Leon Avenue and carried with it the sounds of Decatur. Graham heard the slow rolling tires of Saturday night traffic, the deep bass of music from passing cars, friends shouting back and forth across the boulevard, people playing bocce outside a local pub, and even church bells chiming. He liked these sounds and the freedom he felt away from the art gallery. Being Joel's brother hadn't always been a curse. Graham folded his arms across his chest. It was cold out, and he'd forgotten to bring a jacket.

He didn't want to go home, to the hotel, which was the same place as work. Most of the staff knew him only as Graham Donovan, and they hadn't connected him to the convicted criminal Joel Sapphire. His initial round of investors suggested he change the Sapphire surname to Donovan in court, permanently, but he'd refused. It was enough to be known informally as Graham Donovan. He hadn't introduced himself as Joel Sapphire's brother in seven years.

Graham raised a hand to hail a cab and tried to ignore the clicking of heels on the pavement behind him. A caped figure walked quickly towards him when he turned. He would have gone back to hailing the taxi, except she halted when she saw him, unsure for a moment, then she quickly resumed her graceful stride in his direction. The cape danced around her head and slipped away from her face as she approached. The art gallery was three blocks behind her, and in the distance, the city echoed with the sound of the coming MARTA train.

She seemed like a phantom of the night or a fey creature of the forest, unfazed by the city bustle and noise.

"Wait," she shouted. Her voice rasped and was taken partly by the wind. "Please, wait," she called. "Graham," she tried at last, but not nearly as loud as her previous shouts. At the sound of his name, he lowered his hand. The taxi that slowed in front of him continued down the street.

Ava's breath came in shallow gasps. "I need to know more," she whispered, as though she meant to speak louder but couldn't. "Do you think Joel will try to come after me?"

She coughed and tried to clear her throat. Maybe the cold night air burned her lungs. Graham could almost feel her heart pounding. "We don't have much time to talk," she went on. "My mother has, no doubt, discovered I've escaped and is calling my bodyguard at the very least, and my driver is on his way."

Graham held out his hands. "Joel won't hurt you. I'd stake my life on that."

"But you're not guaranteeing he won't try to find me?"

Graham slumped a little. "No."

"You wanted something from me last night," she said. Her quiet voice held nothing but an innocent statement. He kept his eyes trained on her face, but he knew what she looked like from head to toe. She was more than fully clothed, but the dress he'd seen in the art gallery clung to her curves like a cat suit. He assumed she meant to hide behind all that black fabric, with only her hands and the small moon of her face exposed, but it seemed to emphasis her loveliness. Hair fell across her scarred eye and cheek, but it drew his attention to her lips and the promise of her smile. The woman he wanted to reach out to more than any other woman in the world was the least likely to want him.

And yet . . . she had followed him into the evening street. She stood in front of him like a regal princess. He expected tears, but her eyes were clear and sad.

She tentatively asked again, "What do you want from me?"

He stepped toward her. Graham reached into his pocket and pulled out a picture and handed it to Ava. "Who took this picture?" he asked.

She held the photograph in her hands, but it took several moments for her to realize that she was the woman in the image.

"Where did you get this?" she asked. She stared at the picture as though it were an impossible window to the past.

"Someone sent me photos a few months ago. I don't know who. I've had them analyzed to make certain they're legitimate. No tampering." He hesitated, then, his voice grim, he said, "There are twelve pictures taken in the restaurant that night. Of you and my brother sitting next to each other at the bar. *Talking*."

He pointed to the picture of her and his brother, but all she saw was an image of herself from seven years earlier. She and Joel were sitting at the restaurant bar. Her hair was pulled back into a ponytail. She seemed so young. It was the night she graduated from law school. Joel's arm was looped over the back of her chair. He leaned in; someone might assume he was about to kiss her cheek. Her perfectly flawless, unscarred cheek.

"I've never seen this picture before," she said dully, her voice a rasp. Her hand went to her throat. *But I know what it proves.*

Graham sobered. "Do you remember any more about that night than you did during the trial? You had graduated from law school. You were out with your friends." He moved close to her so they could both see the image at the same time. He pulled out another photo and placed it into her trembling hands.

Graham spoke again, and the urgency disappeared from his voice. "I will take these photos to the authorities, of course. These are grounds for a new trial. I want to find out how many people in that bar were paid to keep quiet about seeing the two of you together. But I don't want you to feel threatened. Tell me you didn't know anything about this. I'm not saying this proves my brother didn't attack you. I want to hear your explanation, Ava. Tell me you couldn't remember meeting my brother that night. Talking to him. Letting some friend of yours take pictures. He says he never met you before that night. He couldn't remember talking to you, he was so drunk. But you weren't drunk; the toxicology reports proved that. Did the trauma of the attack make it impossible to remember—"

"I . . . please." Her voice was a broken whisper.

"I don't know where Joel is or why he's hiding. But I have these pictures. I think he's afraid for his life because of them."

He took the picture from her and slid it inside the breast of his tuxedo jacket. "My brother did not slash your face."

She was angry, confused, and trembling. "He did. Regardless of those pictures. Of any detail . . . Joel did this to me."

"His conviction was purely circumstantial."

"He was found holding me down. He had the knife in his blood-covered hand. He ran when Martin Brown ran out of the restaurant and saw him. Joel did this to me. What you need to tell me is, am I in danger? Is he going to come after me again?" She took a rapid breath that sounded like a low whistle.

"He wouldn't. I'd bet my life on it." Graham knew she should be untouchable, but he wanted to reach out and move the lock of dark hair that fell in front of her face. Her head was turned to the side, and the scars on her left cheek were concealed. He wouldn't forget when she confronted him fully in anger and laughter and forgot to hide the awful lines that marred her face.

"Joel's not coming for you. He's in hiding. Even from me. We're both safe, Ava. The help I want? I want for you to consider for a moment that he might not be guilty. Please. And just tell me the truth about what happened at the restaurant."

Ava stared at him for a long moment with her mouth parted as though she were unable or unwilling to speak. She shook her head, and her hand went to her throat.

"Are you all right?" he asked, and stepped away from the curb.

"I—" she tried to speak but started coughing uncontrollably and quickly stumbled back a few steps. Graham followed her as she opened her purse and shuffled through the contents until a yellow tube emerged, trembled in her hand, and fell to the ground. Graham picked it up and read the label: *Epinephrine. Inject in thigh, through clothes if necessary. Depress plunger and hold for 15 seconds.*

She found a small alcove along a building, pressed her back against the wall, and held out her shaking hand for the tube.

"I . . . need . . . the . . . shot," she gasped.

"Hold on, Ava. Look at me." But her glassy eyes never met

his face. She tried to open her mouth and inhale, but the air didn't go in fast enough. What little air she could pull in created a shrill sound. She tried again and shook her head because the constriction was too great for her.

"Don't panic. I know what to do." He could tell she was trying to control her breathing as he had earlier in the night when she found out he was Joel's brother. Her body shook as she gasped.

"Why do butterflies flutter their wings?" he asked, echoing Nadine's question earlier in the evening. Suddenly her eyes snapped to his. She closed her eyes. Her breathing slowed, but he wasn't sure if she was relaxing or slipping further away. He looked down at the syringe in his hand and sank to his knees before her. He slid his hand into the slit of her skirt and exposed the length of her leg wrapped in black silk nylons. He jabbed the needle deep into the side of her hip, and she stiffened. He paused for a moment before depressing the plunger and releasing the medication into her body.

He counted fifteen seconds and then pulled the syringe from her leg. The contents of her purse were on the sidewalk at his knee. He retrieved an inhaler from her sparse possessions and stood up.

"Open your mouth," he ordered quietly. Ava opened her eyes. She let him put the inhaler between her parted lips. He squeezed the pump, and she huffed a shallow breath. Her eyes never left his. He waited a long moment before giving her another dose. She closed her eyes and inhaled with effort, but Graham could hear the improvement in her breathing.

He rested his head against hers, feeling his own lungs struggling for air.

Graham picked up the items on the ground and piled them back into her purse. Ava was judicious with the things that she carried. Lip balm, keys, wallet, gum. No mirrors. The inhaler and her emergency epinephrine pen.

He put an arm around her waist and helped her walk back to the street.

"Keep your head up. Try to breathe."

He held up his hand, and a taxi appeared like a prayer answered. They were hard to come by anywhere in Atlanta, and especially in Decatur.

"Can you take us to the nearest emergency room?" Graham asked the taxi driver.

"She okay?" the man asked. He had been smiling as he approached, but his happiness faded as he looked at Ava.

"I don't know. She has asthma and also seems to have had an allergic reaction. I don't know if she's okay."

"No, problem. I'll take you."

"No hospitals," Ava struggled. "I can't. Reporters."

"I've got to get you to a doctor. Either I take you in a taxi, or I call an ambulance. They need to tell me you're okay, and then you can go home. Should I call your family?"

"No, don't call my mother, please."

As he guided her into the taxi, Graham felt Ava shivering besides him.

At the shelter, she had reached out to him. She'd offered him food and a place to stay for the night. Graham had been smart and walked away. If he was smart again, he'd put her in the taxi and send her off alone. How would it look if they were seen together like this? What effect might it have on Joel if he saw a news clip of Graham and Ava together?

"I'll go to the hospital," she whispered.

She directed her panicked voice at the window in the taxi cab. Another mirror. She was afraid, and if she stayed with Graham for long, he would take her other places she didn't want to go.

When she met him, did she feel the same way he felt now? She offered him chili and her soft words. Did she want to save him from the cold?

The side of him that could not turn away from responsibility pulled her close and imagined that for this moment, she was his to protect.

"Stay with me, Ava. Don't close your eyes yet, okay?" he said as they sped toward the hospital.

"I need to die," she whispered. *Then I'd stop hating myself.*

Without air, I could sleep.

The medicine created a panicked feeling like she was running and couldn't halt. She shook, not from fear, but adrenaline. When she tried to move, Graham was at her side. When she tried to breathe, she smelled limes.

Limes. Sparkling water and limes. Clean hands, no coat, no loose ends. That was Graham Sapphire. He had an arm around her waist keeping her upright, but Ava got the sense that he was being careful how he touched her. His hand was still and unmoving. She tried to pull away, but her body was a battleground. The allergic reaction combined with stress and asthma to shut down her throat. Her lips and eyes were swollen. The medicine fought to shock her body back into life.

Ava shook like she was cold. She shook like she was afraid. He held her like he could take away the cold and take away the fear. The only reason she might trust him was the years of letters. They didn't convince her that Joel was innocent, but that Graham truly believed in his brother. She gave a reluctant nod of her head at her reflection in the window. Her hair moved like the branches of a weeping willow tree.

Chapter 12

TAXI DRIVERS DIDN'T drive leisurely, but the trip passed by in slow motion. She could see each tree, each building with lights on and people inside. Each breath lasted a minute. In, life. Out, death.

The red neon sign of the emergency room soon lit their path. She wished the driver would turn the car around. She wasn't afraid of death, but in the hospital there was darkness. Her eyes felt heavy, and she needed enough energy to tell the doctors to not let her sleep.

The driver helped Graham pull Ava from the car. She had the strength to stand but not the control to walk without help. She had the sudden urge to laugh.

Graham reached into his pocket and handed the driver several bills.

Ava heard the men exchange a few quick words, and then Graham ushered her through the emergency entrance. They didn't pause long at the registration desk. One look at her swollen face and the nurse escorted them to an exam room.

She tried to keep her eyes open, but they were heavy. She didn't want forced darkness. Her hands strayed to her scars. With her face swelling, she felt a pain along the jagged marks.

The nurse slowly pulled Ava's hands away from her face.

"Ms. Camden, I have to give you another shot and give you a breathing treatment on a nebulizer. What are you allergic to? Nuts? Seafood? Something else?"

"Nuts," she whispered. Then started laughing.

The nurse told Graham it was normal, but the more Ava laughed, the more concerned he seemed.

"I can't stop," Ava explained.

"The medicine creates a high level of anxiety," the nurse

said to Graham. She made Ava lay on a gurney. "She'll come back down in a few minutes. Laughing while she's getting the breathing treatment is probably a good thing. More medicine will get into her lungs. We'll need to get her undressed."

Graham got up to leave.

"You can stay," the nurse offered.

"No. I'm a business colleague. I'm not even her friend. I'm here because she didn't want to call her family."

The nurse sent him out with a few encouraging words. "She'll be fine. Don't worry. You're good to be here. She must trust you."

Ava started laughing again because the nurse could diagnose emotional conditions like trust. The woman helped her into the cold hospital gown and fed her a little cup of syrupy medicine. The second injection made her heart race. Before Ava could react, the nurse put a nebulizer over her nose. The breathing treatment made her lungs open up. She took a breath and counted the ceiling tiles. That was sanity. Ten tiles. The epinephrine and albuterol took effect quickly. She stole a breath of hospital air and returned her own heated exhale. It was like drowning and finally breaking the surface.

"Nice friend," the nurse offered and nodded to the glass door. Graham rocked back on his heels in the hallway. His tuxedo made him seem distant. She liked the jeans and dirty boots. They fit him. The nurse adjusted the mask on Ava's face, and her tentative smile faded as she observed the scars. With the noise of the machine and the mist that danced before her eyes, Ava felt hidden.

"He might be worried, but at least he's not upset with me. My family gets upset easily, and he got stuck helping me out. Wrong place. Wrong time." She tried to turn her face toward the side to hide marks. The nurse told her no.

"Everything is right. Right place. Right time for both of you."

"Are you from Jamaica?" Ava asked, but she knew the answer. The woman had that terrible peace about her that some people were born with. There was no wrong. Everything could be made right. "He used to live there. My friend. He used to live in Jamaica. When he was young. He made a lot of money there. Got his start."

"That white boy?" the nurse asked, letting her accent and smile deepen. "He told you?" Her name was embroidered onto her scrubs and hung around her neck on the hospital security badge. Pearl.

Ava's hand flew to her neck, feeling for her grandmother's necklace. A prayer for each bead. Pearl pointed to a folded pile of clothes on the chair and picked up the jewelry. Ava's one hundred and two prayers were there. The nurse put the long necklace into the bed next to Ava's trembling hand.

Please God, don't let me fall asleep.

"He told me all about himself in letters," Ava said. She knew him more than he realized. "Even when he thought I would never answer."

I never knew what he looked like. I wanted to hate him. He asked me to believe something I can't. I read his letters because he was like me. He was angry, too.

Ava wanted the nurse to say Graham must have trusted her to have written so many letters, but the woman only shut down the machine, wrapped up the mask, and checked her vital signs.

"You have relatives from the islands?" the nurse asked.

"My grandfather, my dad's dad, was from Jamaica. My mom's people are from Savannah. Seems like I should belong to the water, but here I am in Atlanta, among the trees."

"Not all of Jamaica is by the water, you know. The best part of the whole country is the mountains, but everyone thinks about the beach because you can see it. The mountains are beautiful because you have to find them." The nurse looked at her watch. "We need to check on you for another hour, monitor your breathing and oxygen levels. Then you can go home. I'll send your friend back in."

The nurse found Graham down the hall. When she returned with him, they stood just outside the examination cubicle. Ava watched as the woman spoke to him for a long time. They took turns smiling at each other. What did the nurse say to make him smile? What did he say to earn the same back? The two embraced. The nurse had known him for only a few minutes. His warmth was magnetic. He radiated strength.

Ava closed her eyes and saw the events of the evening in reverse. She thought she saw Graham take a business card from the taxi driver. The entire night in the gallery he'd barely spoken to anyone. But he felt comfortable with the taxi driver and the nurse. These people could be his friends. He moved easily among people who worked at night. Among people of every social level, every culture and race.

When he came back into the exam room, his smile was gone. "Are you going to call your sister?" She shook her head. "Mother?"

"I'm fine." *I had an accident, but now I'm fine.* "You can go home."

"Do you really want to stay here alone?" he asked.

"Do you really want to be here?" she returned.

"How about we follow your rules from the shelter? No lying."

She paused. She would count the ceiling tiles, even the divided ones. "No, I don't want to be here alone. But I don't mind being alone."

"Was that so difficult?"

Ava couldn't think of the last time she'd told the truth to anyone but him. It was difficult. Being honest meant being vulnerable. Could you be honest and still be on your guard?

"How about you? Why won't you go home?"

"I'd be worried about you if I left. That's the truth," Graham said. "Pearl is working on your discharge papers. That could take awhile, so you might as well enjoy a little nap."

He sat in the only chair in the room, but he turned it away from the bed and faced the door. She didn't want to sleep, except that resting her eyes seemed tempting.

She closed them for a moment then was jarred awake by the sensation of falling. She drifted in and out of sleep like someone jumping on and off a train. There had to be a better way. A clock showed that only thirty minutes had passed.

Graham sat with his elbows on his knees. He didn't have his phone out. He wasn't reading a magazine.

"I've been asleep?" she asked, and sat up. Her clothes were neatly folded on a chair, along with her cape. In lieu of snatching it onto the gurney and wrapping herself like a mummy, she pulled a blanket as high as she could. The hospital gown felt very thin.

"Yes." He nodded and turned back to the door. "Does this happen to you a lot? These allergy attacks? Asthma attacks? Either-or?"

"Never," she said. *No lying.* "Rarely," she amended.

"What would have happened if I wasn't with you? You might have collapsed right there on the street."

"I usually pick up the warning signs earlier. But I was distracted tonight." She leaned back in bed with only her eyes moving. If she were outside, she'd be counting stars. "How did you know what to do?"

"Joel was allergic to everything when we were growing up. Peanuts, shrimp, you name it. He had a few incidents, and I watched out for him when my mother was working. Going to the hospital was not an option. We didn't have the money. Being sick wasn't an option. It didn't do us any good to show any weakness in my old neighborhood. We needed to stay quiet and blend in."

Blending in would mean fitting in, and Ava wondered how he had ever done that in his life. She tilted her head downward to make her hair cover her face.

"Don't do that." He moved to stand beside the bed. His shoes were silent. His quiet, quieted her. "Open your mouth again. I need to see if the swelling is going down." She parted her lips, but her tongue was very dry. Graham brought a cup of ice water with a straw to her mouth.

She drank until it was empty.

"That was the most delicious thing I've ever tasted." On the ceiling were those ten perfect tiles. One for each complete year Joel should have served in prison.

Graham refilled the cup and left it on the table next to her.

Then he backed away until he reached the wall and turned toward the door. She wished she could help him escape.

"Do you want to talk about the pictures of me and your brother?" she asked.

"No. Not while you're in the hospital."

"You are going to stand there in silence?"

"I like silence. Do you really want to talk while you're still barely able to breathe? As much as I need answers from you, not at the expense of your life."

Ava lay there fighting a wave of shame.

The cardiology wing of this hospital is named after my father. If we walked there through the deserted hospital corridors, another portrait of him would be waiting for us. He would hate you, the way I should but can't figure out how.

I haven't been in a hospital since my niece Lydia was born. I heard her cry through the closed delivery room door. When they brought her out, her eyes were staring at me, even though she was too new to the world to focus. She loved me without seeing me. When Lexi was born, I was afraid to come back to the hospital. I waited for her birth at my sister's house and watched Lydia and washed baby clothes and matched socks. Pink with pink. Blue with blue.

I'm used to being outside at night. I'm not afraid of the hospital. I'm afraid of the walls. And the ceiling. And darkness without sky. It feels strange that I can't see the stars.

I have to tell you the truth, Graham.

Ava liked silence, but she wanted to hear his voice. He made no sound. He stood without shifting or rocking. There wasn't a bit of nerves about him. There must have been things he wanted to say, too.

"I want you to set up a meeting between your brother and me," she said.

"I swear to you, I don't know where he is, and I can't promise the impossible anymore."

"What's that supposed to mean?"

Graham debated his answer. *My mother is dying. She has cancer. I promised her I'd find him. Just as I promised her years ago I'd clear his name. It appears that neither of those promises will be kept, at least not in time for her to know it.* He turned to look at Ava. "I'm not going to destroy you to get the truth. Go home. Go back to your work at the shelter. That's all that matters. The end."

"No, it doesn't matter. My mother has cancelled the lease on the building. In six weeks, there will be no more shelter." Ava rubbed the subtle roughness of a pearl between her fingers then moved to the next.

Please God, don't let The Light House close down.

He frowned. "What? Why?"

"She doesn't think it is safe for me. She wants me to work at the law firm. She wants me to get over my scars. And I admit that I have some things to work out, but the shelter isn't some dangerous way of acting out my issues. I've made promises, too, Graham. That shelter is my redemption."

The obvious question hung in the silence between them. *Redemption for what?*

Graham took a deep breath and looked up at the ceiling. Was he wishing for stars, or did he count the ceiling tiles?

"The shelter should stay open. That has nothing to do with you or Joel or your mother. It's for those people who need it." He exhaled a long sigh. "I could help you keep it open."

His gaze settled on her, dark and intense. Ava felt a seed of fear rising in her chest, but she pushed it down and tried to bring back up her anger. She wasn't afraid of the night or blood or death, but she was afraid of his eyes when they met hers. She needed the anger. The anger allowed her control and power.

"I want to see the case files and all of those pictures you have," she said. "I want access to everything you have on my attack."

"Fine. You look at the pictures. Tell me what happened between you and Joel that night and why you never admitted it. But you can't meet with my brother, even if I do find him alive. And I'll help you with the shelter. Agreed?"

"Agreed. Should we shake hands?"

"No." He kept his hands in his pockets. "I don't make promises anymore."

She reluctantly put down the hand she had extended and picked up her necklace. Ava spun it around her finger like a noose.

Please God, let me forgive him when he realizes his brother truly is the one who slashed my face. Nothing I can tell him about that night changes that fact.

"Fine. No promises. I don't want to wait any longer to talk about the night Joel attacked me." She pushed the call button for the nurse.

Chapter 13

GRAHAM TRIED TO decipher the emotion that haunted Ava's solitary mansion in one of the city's oldest and most exclusive neighborhoods. The gates like the open mouth of a beast. The imposing windows were angry eyes. Trees lined the long driveway, each pine tree a sentinel. A rock wall guarded the perimeter. In a few spots, stones had broken and fallen away. *Something there is that doesn't love a wall*, Graham thought.

They walked through the two rooms at the front of the house, a parlor and grand dining room. Both were empty of furniture. All that remained were the dark hardwood floors and closed drapes—the same heavy drapery used in hotels to keep out the light. He'd never been in a large home he wanted to describe as suffocating and oppressive. *Gothic*, he decided. The way the curtains were drawn made him feel like they were always drawn, not only at night.

As soon as they started down the hallway, Ava paused and slipped off her shoes, silencing her steps. Her quiet feet lacked nail polish. Graham followed her silence. It was another way for her to disappear. "I would sell this place and use the money for the shelter," she said over her shoulder as she walked. "But it's part of a trust controlled by my family. My grandfather built it."

They arrived at an ornate set of doors that were a wooden replica of Rodin's *The Gates of Hell*, and Ava pushed them open to reveal a dimly lit library. Ava pressed a button on the wall, and the room illuminated with light from above. A gas-powered fireplace blazed into life. If he were a child, he would have believed it magic. Considering the entrance again, and the books and the firelight, he'd been mistaken. Not Hell. He'd walked through the doors of paradise.

He was the enemy and she the victim, but her library

seemed like a sanctuary to him. Since he'd met her at the shelter, he had been in a constant state of longing. Hoping to see her again. Hoping to hear her voice. But now, all he had to look forward to was another angry exchange.

As children, he and Joel would hide in the shelves at the public library. They had nowhere else to go after school—not on days when their father was at home, drunk—so Mother would pick them up there when she got off work. That was where you learned to be quiet. You can't be taught silence. It has to be in you. They were big and rough boys, but they loved to lose themselves in volumes of books. Sometimes they wouldn't read. They would open the books and close their eyes and make up their own stories.

The oak shelves in the Camden library were built into the walls. The main section held leather volumes that must have been handed down from the generations of Camdens that preceded Ava. He turned to the other walls and noticed that the library was not only leather-bound classics or hardback literature. There were children's books, paperback books, romance novels, and westerns. Everything that could be read lined the walls.

Graham suddenly realized he'd immersed himself in the library while Ava remained at the entrance. The light from the hallway illuminated her back and kept her face in the shadows.

"I'll be back in a few minutes with tea," she said.

THE DELICATE AROMA of bergamot filled the room.

He preferred the bitterness of coffee. It was the one thing he got from his father that Graham wasn't ashamed of. Walter Sapphire had worked at the front desk of broken-down hotels whenever he was sober enough. Graham's mother, Wendy, had worked every job she could get. Coffee house, daycare, diner. She had dreamed of being a chef one day. Odd hours meant coffee brewed any time of day. Graham never imagined that his life might lead him to Ava Camden and this tranquil cup of tea.

He went to college late, slowly earning tuition money

renovating and reselling homes in the neighborhood where he grew up. It had once been a bad neighborhood, and he and his brothers played with the local kids. Only a few were white. Most of them black, some of them immigrants, all of them poor. Drug addicts and alcoholics wandered the streets. He and Joel promised each other to never drink, never to be like their dad. Joel paid a high price for breaking that promise.

Having tea was a reminder that he was no longer that same poor little kid from the streets. He looked at the room and books and exhaled. He was a kid who relied on his strength and his fists and periodically getting a worn paperback book to keep him safe. There were only a few things that allowed him and his brother to escape from the angry hands of their father.

Ava moved to the seat across from him and pulled her hair back. She turned to face Graham and exposed her scars.

"Seven years ago, I was beaten unconscious and left for dead outside a restaurant in Atlanta. Doctors put two hundred and four stitches into my face. Two years ago, my father died. I didn't cry when they stitched my face, and I didn't cry when they put him in the ground, because I was angry at him for what he asked me to do during the trial. And angry at myself. I told myself that it didn't change your brother's guilt. I still believe that."

Graham set his cup down. "I just want the truth."

"The first and only time I spoke to Joel was that night. I had just graduated from law school. I'd eaten dinner and decided to sit at the restaurant's bar. I didn't drink. I had a soda with lime. Joel sat down next to me. He seemed shy; he had trouble with words. I felt sorry for him. But he seemed to be a good listener."

"He was," Graham said.

"He started drinking. It was clear he didn't have much experience with it. I was worried about him. I tried to distract him. So did the bartender. She pretended to be a fortune teller. The details are fuzzy, now. Nothing stands out as profound. We talked about books. And Joel drank more."

"He was worried about living up to our expectations of him," Graham said quietly.

"I talked to the bartender about calling a cab for him, and she agreed she'd take care of him. I gave him a hug, and he hugged me back. He was drunk. He was slurring his words, but he seemed cheerful. 'Congratulations on law school, Ava: congratulations on your football career, Joel. I'll be watching you on television,' that kind of thing. Then, I left." Ava took a long swallow of tea. Her hands shook. "The rest is history," she added.

"That's all?" Graham asked. "I have a dozen photographs of the two of you in deep conversation and laughing and the hug. And it was all innocent bar talk?"

"Yes."

"I don't understand why you lied about it, Ava."

When your brother didn't tell investigators anything about our conversation—couldn't remember even meeting me, because he was drunk—my father made sure no one would ever find out."

"He bribed witnesses?"

Ava nodded. "And he told me I could never admit it. That it would only raise questions. Innuendo about a possible relationship. That it had no impact on Joel Sapphire's guilt or innocence." She hesitated. Then, "That I'd already done enough to drag the family name into the spotlight."

"My God."

"It doesn't change the fact that Joel got drunk and attacked me."

"That sweet guy who hugged you in the bar had no reason to turn into a monster."

"Maybe I reminded him of an old girlfriend. Maybe he's the kind of drinker who goes into sudden rages."

Graham went very still. The thought in his brain was painfully unwelcome. *Like our father.*

"Can I see the rest of the pictures now?" she asked.

"You can have them. You have no idea who might have taken them?"

"None. There might have been camera flashes going off. People taking pictures with their phones. But I had no reason to think someone was photographing me and Joel."

He rubbed his hands over his face. "I am desperate. For reasons you can't understand." He thought of his mother and how she didn't for a moment mourn the loss of her hair. How she never felt ugly when they removed both her breasts. How telling her Joel was innocent might be the one thing that could save her life when surgery and chemo had failed them all. Ava didn't need to know about his desperation.

"I don't need your pity any more than you need mine," he whispered. "But I do need your help. I'm asking for eight weeks of your time, maybe less, maybe four, because we might not need that long—" He wanted to punch something, likely his brother, the next time he saw him. "I don't know what the next couple of months might bring. If things change"—*If my mother dies*—"there will be no need to continue our acquaintance."

"You want me to help you clear Joel's name," Ava said grimly, "even though I have the scars to prove that he did it."

"The scars are fading, and maybe the certainty of Joel's guilt will fade, too."

"You expect me to believe that?" Her voice was like a dagger. Something that pierced him with shame, both accusing him and convicting him of a different kind of crime. "He carved open my face on purpose. I was left in a pool of my blood. I wear his guilt on my face."

She turned her face further into the light. There were three long gashes from her left cheek to her forehead. He had seen the slashes before from the crime scene photos. They didn't look like they were made by human hands, but rather a wild and determined animal. His intent stare made her furrow her brow. He could assure her that his stares were not at the scars, but at the fact that another human being had done this horrible thing to her.

Her eyes were coal black and matched the onyx hair that surrounded her face. She looked exhausted, not just from the current night, but the sum total of all the nights before her. Graham wished he could ease the stress or say words to have her soften toward him. But he could only say, "Joel couldn't have done this to you. He gets sick at the sight of blood. Even a drop. He has never hurt a living soul in his life."

"I've heard this all before. He was the star athlete with the heart of gold. He was the autistic son. A little whimsical but always dependable. Until this."

"We take your attack and your injuries very seriously."

"No, you don't. What have you been doing these past seven years, Mr. Sapphire? Making more money."

"Taking care of my mother and trying to get my wrongly accused brother released from jail."

"As much as you want to prove Joel is innocent, I want to prove that he is guilty. Why is he hiding from the world? Have you so conveniently forgotten that your family's initial attempt to free your brother involved slandering my name? Security footage of my dress was shown. It was too short. Oh, your attorneys even called up my classmates, asked them why I wasn't like normal girls. I wasn't normal, was I? I was a rich, spoiled tease. I had done something to deserve this. I think the defense attorneys were being kind when they referred to me as 'a repressed slut,' or, on bad days, what was I? Oh, yes. I remember now. *A whore*," she said.

His lips pressed together to form a thin line as she continued her onslaught.

"In court and in the media, they showed pictures of my slashed face and called me a whore," she repeated, and her voice trembled. "You can see that I have no reason to trust you or your family."

Graham nodded. "At the same time, my construction company was hit by a flurry of frivolous lawsuits. I nearly lost everything. Clients walked away. Doors were shut in my face. Your family—your father—tried to ruin me, my business, my family. My mother was hospitalized five times due to the stress. Every week for months she was hit in the face with stories in the media about Joel, about our family, about my father. Dirt, lies, gossip. I hated the tactics Harvey Joyce used in defending Joel, but he told me it was the only hope we had. I told myself the end justified the means, that we'd clear Joel and find out who really attacked you. I believed, we honestly believed, the police would find your true attacker before the case ever went to trial. We would have done anything to save Joel. We waited one year for that trial, but it only took *one week* to convict him."

"That week felt like centuries to me," she said.

"Every trial analyst tried to prosecute Joel with a hate crime, because you were black and he was white. He was convicted before we went to trial. You met him. You knew that wasn't the truth. He wasn't a racist."

"How would I know that? I only spoke to him for an hour."

Ava let her hair fall back over her scars. Talking was over. She got up. He barely heard her feet touch the floor as she paced back and forth. It was the sound of a metronome or ticking time bomb. She had a thousand reasons to hate Joel and only one reason to hate Graham. "This isn't for me or Joel. It's for you, too. You need closure," Graham said.

She turned on him, her scars paling in sharp relief against her brown skin. "You don't know what I need. You want my help, my trust, and all I get in exchange is flashbacks to the night I was almost killed. And I get to start having my murder fantasies again. Does that shock you? Well, it shouldn't. I've imagined killing your brother in a thousand ways. My mother thinks I'm insane, and half of the time she is right. Normal women want pretty dresses or a trip to the spa, and I want to take a knife to Joel's face and his heart. Are you sure I'm the right person to help you?"

"Would you lie to me again?" he asked.

"Yes," she said. "I lie all the time to protect my sanity."

"Are you afraid of me?"

"No," she said. The word came out quickly and surprised Graham.

"Then I do need your help."

"I need to know you aren't only working to find justice for your brother. You are actually looking for the truth, and that truth might be he is guilty. I need proof you are really trying to help both of us. How far are you willing to go to save your brother, Mr. Sapphire?" She let her eyes fall to the hard wall of his chest. "Would you really do anything?"

He followed the small movement of her hand to the table next to her. She had brought in a tray with cups and a teapot and a knife.

Chapter 14

AVA HELD OUT a carving knife. She pointed it at him.

"My heart races every night. I don't know if it's fear or anger or panic. Certain nights I think I'm going to die. I wish I would die. I feel a hand holding my face to the ground. Time hasn't made it hurt any less. What if we made a pinky promise? What if I pricked your finger? Do you think it would make me hurt less?"

She walked slowly toward him.

"What if I wanted to cut your face? Ladies love a man with a scar. Would you let me put this knife against your face? Do you trust me? How far are you willing to go to prove that your brother is innocent?"

He stood, but calmly. She advanced on him, but he didn't back away. "What if you took off your shirt?" She pressed the knife to his tuxedo jacket. The firelight caused a flash of reflection. She traced a line along his collar bone from shoulder to throat. He didn't flinch.

He spoke in a whisper. "Cut me if you want. I understand why you want to hurt me."

He grabbed her hand and brought the knife close to his throat. Ava stumbled toward him.

"You are angry at me for being Joel's brother. I'm angry at him, too. Is it my face or my body you want to scar?"

When she didn't answer, he tossed her hand away and started to unbutton his shirt. One of his silver cufflinks skidded to the floor as he shrugged out of both the shirt and his jacket. Her eyes took in the broad expanse of his chest and the faint covering of dark hair that trailed down his abdomen. He was beauty. He was lean muscle and smooth skin. Ava's hand started to fall to her side. She noticed two marks on his perfect body. A

Greek letter branded into the side of his bicep and a terrible burn mark at the top of one hip.

"I'm surprised that you don't like my scars," he said. "Certainly a knife wouldn't hurt as much as a burn. And you aren't my family or even a friend, so why would it hurt?" His voice was clipped. He stepped toward her, and she backed away. "I've never been cut before. Be gentle with me."

She shook her head. The section of burned skin at his waist disappeared into his pants. It was an odd location. Not like a hand that might accidentally touch a hot stove.

"I got that when I was nine. My father had already knocked me down a couple of times, and I kept getting up. He wanted to punish me in a way that I would remember. Bruises heal. Broken bones mend. He decided to burn me with an iron while my mother and brother watched. Joel was five years old; he doesn't remember. They were the ones who screamed. Not me. My father held the iron to my skin until I passed out. All I could think is that if I could endure the pain, he wouldn't kill my mother and Joel.

"We all have scars, Ava. Just because mine are hidden doesn't make them any less painful. Whenever someone looks at me, I feel their eyes on my skin where bruises used to be. I would never have approached you if I thought my brother could have done this to you. Never. He couldn't. He would never. He saw what our father did to me and our mom. I understand why you like to hide. My attacker was a man who was supposed to have loved me. But I understand if you want to make me pay. If you need to use your knife on me, I'm not afraid."

He reached for her hand again and put the knife to his chest. When she resisted and tried to pull back, he held her hand firmly and made a slow slash across his chest. The cut was thin and superficial, but blood began dripping along the wound.

He let go of her hand. Her eye went from the slash on his chest to the red on her knife. Graham wiped the line of blood off his chest with a finger. More red dripped down. She looked like she'd never seen blood before.

"Pinky promise?" he offered.

Ava stepped back. She didn't like the silence. His words were echoing in her head.

We all have scars.

She had lived in her perfect hate and anger. She'd never considered that everyone else had their own worlds of anger and hate.

What did I do?

"Ava?" he asked in a low voice. "I'm sorry. I shouldn't have done that."

Her back found the edge of a bookcase, and she slid down and curled into a ball. Her head dropped into her hands.

"Butterflies flutter their wings so they can fly," she said into her hands. He needed to leave. She didn't want him to see her like this. Like she was losing control. "Get away from me. Get dressed and get out," she ordered again.

She heard the sounds of him dressing. It was a quiet rustling of shirt and jacket. She wondered if he was being deliberately slow. She felt tears stinging in her eyes. She was going crazy. How could she both despise him and also despise hurting him?

He moved forward and crouched in front of her. "I'm calling your sister. You don't need to be alone. I'm sorry."

She exploded, unable to conceal her tear filled eyes. "Get out of my house and leave the pictures. Get out. Get out." In her mind she screamed for him to leave and stay a thousand times. Her head sank back into her palms as he left. She didn't need Joel to destroy when she had Graham.

What had happened to her dreams of a normal life? She had wanted to be a lawyer, an artist, fall in love, have a family, but now she wanted to see the dangerous side of life. She looked out the window and noticed the wild oak tree in the center of the backyard. Its long branches were forever reaching for her, but it had been struck by lightning years before. The tree reached for her, but it was already dead.

She saw the shadow of her father in the corner of library. Did he want her to join him, or did he warn her away? She needed to get out of the house before more ghosts came to haunt her.

She heard Graham leave, and his absence made more tears fall. On the table was the stack of pictures of her before. Her at twenty-four and desperate to die. Smiling, perfect, and unhappy. Seven years ago was the time before Lydia and Lexi. Before Nadine's new lightning bolt hairstyle and her sunshine filled house. It was before her awkward brother-in-law Craig became her additional protector. Her mother did not buy Ava pretty dresses in those days or fix her up on funny blind dates. Lance Bertram would have been sitting on a park bench strung out. Howard would have been too drunk to listen to a sermon at Peachtree Missions. Her father would have still been alive.

She thought back to the brand on Graham's arm. Ava could not remember seeing another white man wearing that emblem. The mark of his fraternity was the same Greek letter that her father bore.

"You earn it. No matter what, once you have this mark, you have a place to belong," Cecil Camden would say.

We want to see your scar. When you're not here, we don't remember what you look like.

Ava tried to remember her father's smile. It was lost to her. She remembered riding on his back as a child. Her hand strayed to that keloid scar that felt smooth to the touch. She hadn't understood until she went to college how exactly her father had earned that Greek letter. To Ava, the symbol was a word with a mathematical function and a meaning in church. She tried to reconcile the difference between the letter and the wound. How could an injury, with a long history of marking criminals and slaves, be considered a sign of brotherhood?

She touched the scars on her face. They were the opposite of her father's and Graham's scars. Hers were deep and not raised. Hers were jagged and not smooth. She was in a sisterhood of one. She would be forever sorry that she had threatened Graham with the knife. She wasn't insane. She didn't want to hurt him. She would pay him back for that blood.

Ava peeked out into the dark room. She wasn't afraid of ghosts or memories, but she saw a flash of light. A terrible reminder of Graham's absence. One of his silver cufflinks still sat on the table near the chair. Where was the other? Her eyes scoured the room. She heard no sirens or warning bells, but she got up and put on her coat. A reflective glow like a lightning bolt caught her eye. In a dark corner on the floor, Graham's second cufflink glimmered like a beacon of possibility.

A voice came to her from the past. A voice she'd completely forgotten. Was it Joel's or someone else's? She couldn't tell. Words her attacker whispered as he pressed the knife into her face.

Lay still. Once she sees your *face, she'll know better than to flirt with other men again.*

Chapter 15

AT TWO HOURS until sunrise, Ava stood next to Brad Vargas on the dock at Lake Clara Meer in Piedmont Park. There was always a gothic feel to the old setting, as if the stone walls and gazebos might suddenly shimmer with Victorian ghosts. The dark mirror of water had a thin film of autumn pollen on the surface. As the paramedics entered the lake, the water rippled around the body floating in the distance.

Good morning, Heartache.

In a significant example of fate or irony, when she looked across the vast green space and its forest, she knew that Graham's mother lived in one of the lovely old neighborhoods that bordered the park. Their lives were connecting with invisible threads.

Ava stood on the embankment and handed her camera to Brad.

"I'm not here to take pictures," she said.

The victim was a white male. His clothes were folded into a neat pile on the embankment. He'd gone into the water on purpose. Confusion. Overdose. Suicide. They turned over the thin body. He'd been an athlete, and the roundedness of youth had long left him.

Hold your breath for as long as you can. You can't breathe water. You will have to hurt. You will have to die sometime. Only jump if you can fly. Don't you know that drowning is like flying? You can fly, water angel, now you can fly forever.

"Appears to be around twenty years old. I can't imagine he had anything on him worth stealing. Someone called the station earlier about a man running down the middle of 10th Street. This must be him. If we'd found him sooner, he'd still be alive."

Brad sighed. He didn't like seeing the dead any more than she did. They shared so many ghosts, including her father's. She'd found Cecil Camden on the floor of his office and called 911. Brad heard the news through police reports and came by the hospital in time to wade into their family crisis. Sera had been like a wildcat. She refused to see her dead husband's body. She would not let anyone get close to her except Brad. She felt a solemn gratitude to him after Ava's attack and trial. Law was the one thing her mother respected. Brad consoled her mother in the cold, overly bright waiting room, while Ava and Nadine sat by their father's body in a private room, holding hands.

In those first hours, even their mother was lost to them. They'd been completely orphaned for days until Sera re-emerged. Beautiful black dress, high heels, a little lipstick and mascara. Those were the things she needed to make the world right.

The world could not always be made right. It was upside down, and you had to learn to live in that snow globe, sitting on the clouds, letting snowflakes gather around you, and seeing the city skyline above you.

Ava pointed to the camera. "Do you need any of those images?" she asked.

He told her no but still clicked through the pictures. Ava turned her back to the display while Brad cataloged what she'd photographed over the years.

"Car wreck. Botched robbery. Dispute between neighbors. Stray bullet. Fire. Robbery.

Homicide. That one from yesterday, carjacking gone wrong, feels like a lifetime ago. We caught her boyfriend a few hours later. It turns out that she was pregnant. He didn't want the baby."

Ava walked to the end of the dock. The water wasn't deep. It was murky and without the moonlight, and she couldn't see her face.

Don't jump if you can't fly.

"There should be a name for mother and baby ghosts that enter heaven at the same time," she said this to the lake. The night her father died. She wanted to die, too.

"*Los abrazados?* The embraced?" Brad offered behind her. He picked up two pinecones and tossed them into the water. They fell into the lake without making a sound, but eventually the ripples would reach the shore. "What do you want to do with these?" he asked. He held out the camera but did not walk toward her or the edge of the dock. He wanted her to return.

Ava went back to him. He'd always been a badge and a warning, but she'd forgotten how he treated her mother with kindness. Brad could understand Sera's wildness and rage and anger. Ava noticed a small scar on his lip.

We all have scars.

"I'm getting rid of the pictures."

"That's a good start. Your mother called me. Told me Joel's brother is bothering you. She wants a restraining order. Do I need to have a talk with him? You know, off the record?"

"No. I was hoping to talk to *you* off-record. Off the record from my mother. And off-record from your official role as a police officer."

"Okay. Wait here a few minutes. Let me tie up some loose ends, and I'll be back."

Brad went to the paramedics. They would cart the body away, and the park would belong to the living again. In another hour, even though it would still be night, the park would fill with morning runners and boot camp exercise groups. She'd always been suspicious of that early morning camaraderie, but if everyone had scars, maybe there was healing in the hours that brought daybreak. Maybe there was healing in running when nothing chased you.

Ava sat on a stone wall near the water and started calculating the number of bricks on the wall. She paused to listen to a bird chirping and lost track of her calculations. Something is there that does love a wall.

"Are you absolutely convinced there weren't any other viable suspects who might have attacked me? Anyone other than Joel Sapphire?" she asked when Brad returned.

"Technically, yes. No one saw Joel actually cut you. Even

Martin Brown, the guy who ID'd Joel, only saw Joel huddled over you. Why the questions?"

"Joel's brother believes someone else was there that night."

"Of course he does."

"It was your case, Vargas. Is there anything you would have done differently? My dad and the media made a circus of the case." She looked at him pointedly. He knew. Of course he knew what her father had done.

"I wouldn't have changed anything. And, yes, your father put undue pressure on the prosecution. The media makes a circus of every high profile trial. Joel was at the scene of the crime. He was holding the bloody knife. He didn't give us reason to think he'd been framed. He said almost nothing about that night. No memories. Like you. His only defense was, "I couldn't have done this," but that's not enough when you're holding a weapon, covered in blood, and don't know how you got there."

"Do you know anything about his brother, Graham?" Ava asked.

"Grew up on the southside. It was a rough neighborhood. What we see downtown, even over by the shelter, is nothing compared to where he grew up. Some of their associates were known criminals, but petty stuff. Burglary. Some of their associates did well. Stayed out of trouble. Went on to college. Did all right for themselves. It couldn't have been easy growing up as two little white boys in the hood."

"Father tried to smear Graham. Tried to ruin his reputation as a businessman."

"Yep. Never found much to use against him, not really. If I recall, Graham was a hustler as a kid, paper route and odd jobs. He worked in construction. He learned to build and renovate before he graduated from high school. Now he's got these hotels and money. A real Cinderella story."

"What about anything weird during the trial? Did anything not add up right?"

"I guess the only thing that bothered me is that there were no character witnesses for Joel. The defense named several people, but none of them came forward. It was rumored he was friends with the governor's daughter in college, but when they talked to her, she said she didn't know him. The way the media played it, their black friends from the old neighborhood didn't want to stand up for Joel. Maybe it was because he was white, and they felt they couldn't side with him over you even if he was a friend. Other people say his old friends were jealous when he got drafted to play football. Usually someone comes forward to defend a guy. All Joel had was his family. No one else."

"What does your gut tell you?" Ava asked.

"If Joel did it, he was so drunk or high, he wasn't planning it, he wasn't competent, and he isn't likely to do something like that again—if he stays sober. If he's innocent . . . hell, I don't think he's innocent. I think he made a mistake. Maybe the media played him up to be a menace, full of hate, a danger to women. But that I don't believe. I do believe, though, that he was capable of doing it in a psycho fit."

"Have you ever arrested a person and wondered if you got the right guy?"

"Never."

"Am I crazy for talking to his brother?"

"No, Ava. You aren't crazy. Taking pictures of crime scenes is crazy, but I understand what you are doing. If you keep talking to Graham Sapphire, I want you to be careful. You've been walking some strange paths these past seven years. It seems like what you want is to relive the past. I was there. I'm here now, too. I can help you if you let me."

Brad put his hand on top of hers. It was a gesture like he could take away her cold, but he couldn't.

Ava pulled her hand away carefully. "You're angry at me all the time. And you have a wife. You really aren't a good choice for a friend."

"My wife and I have been estranged for some time."

"Probably cheating on her hasn't made you the best husband."

"I have never cheated on her. I might flirt with you—"

"And my mother. And Nadine. And every other—"

"—but you aren't ever going to take me up on my offer. Are

you?" he asked. His voice was hopeful, but his eyes looked at her scars.

"No," she said.

"I'm like you, Ava. I'm angry at everyone. Like you're angry. This isn't the easiest line of work. I have a bad habit of being angry. I'm sorry about that. But you shouldn't be out at night. You shouldn't treat your amazing life like it's worthless."

"And is working at the homeless shelter worthless?"

"Yes. I'm not saying the shelter should be closed, but it is beneath you."

"Nothing is beneath me."

"Look at how you live. Your house is an empty castle. Five families could live there. You shouldn't be slopping hash to bums. You asked me what I think. You didn't ask me for what you wanted to hear."

"You are right, Brad. I want to hear that you and Elaine are happy. I want to hear that working at the shelter is a good thing. I want to hear happy things. Maybe I am changing. Maybe I'm right to relive the past." She stared into the dark water. "Who knows the most about that night?" she asked. She'd told Brad about the photographs. "It has to be the person who took the pictures of me and Joel."

"I can talk to Martin Brown for you. He was the night manager."

"Let me think about it."

If Ava was honest with herself, which she rarely was, she was the one who knew the most. Details of that night had been buried in the fog of terror and pain. She'd gone to sit at the bar because she had no one to talk to. Joel, quirky, sweetly shy, had befriended her. There were a lot of pieces missing from that night, because she let them get lost.

"I don't know about talking to Martin," she said. She was lying again. Brad didn't care about lies. She thanked him for his time, took her camera, and walked away.

The bartender had been a petite woman. Beautiful face, dramatic tattoos. She told the police the restaurant was so busy she didn't recall seeing Ava or Joel that night. Father had paid her to make sure she didn't change her story.

Ava had spent seven years trying to forget that night. Now she halted on the path and deleted all the photos from her camera. It was empty, like the lake behind her, only a home to ghosts.

THE BARTENDER WAS good at her job. She seemed to understand her customers' lonely moods. Ava—the recent law grad, Joel—the newly drafted professional football player. The woman offered a few jokes, congratulations, words of encouragement. She'd been kind and funny. She said she loved books and could tell people their fortunes by quoting lines from novels. Ava was surprised to hear how well-read Joel was, the brawny athlete. Ava quizzed the bartender for a line of fortune for each of them.

The bartender said her own fortune was: *Learn from my miseries, and do not seek to increase your own.*

They took turns trying to guess the novels the bartender quoted lines from.

Joel's fortune was, *The scent of bitter almonds always reminded him of the fate of unrequited love.*

As the evening progressed, the bar grew busier, and the bartender grew distant and tense. Ava noticed that the manager was helping out, scowling. The bartender stopped smiling and talking and telling them fortunes from books.

That was the same time Joel became noticeably drunk. Ava put down a large tip, made sure the bartender would call a cab for him, hugged him, then got up to leave. She'd been drinking sparkling water with limes. It was her favorite drink. It made her look social but allowed her to stay sober.

She thanked the bartender as she left. "Are you okay?" Ava asked.

The woman smiled differently than before. It was the smile of someone braced for pain, not happiness. "I'm fine. I'm great," she said with awkward cheerfulness. "I forgot to give you your last quote."

Have all beautiful things sad destinies?

AVA SHOOK HER head, sorting through the strange pieces of those memories. As she walked on, a jogger ran past and said, "Good morning."

Be thankful you are alive.

Chapter 16

WENDY SAPPHIRE didn't like cut flowers. She enjoyed living things, like plants. She adored football, and she also loved romance novels. Since life lacked happily-ever-afters, she sought fairy tale endings in books. Graham let himself into his mother's house carrying a potted African violet and a stack of new paperbacks. The covers showed shirtless Vikings, a few highland warriors, and an English rake or two. The woman in the bookstore had given him a nod of approval when he admitted the novels were for his mother.

"Smart woman," the bookseller said.

He wondered if it was smart to wish for happiness.

I feel a hand holding my face to the ground.

I had an accident, but now I'm fine.

What happened to those who could not find happy endings? Everywhere Graham turned he found loose ends that could not be tied.

Wendy sat in the sunroom, greeting him with half-closed eyes and a smile toward the brightening sky. She wore a pale blue dress better suited for a summer dance, and her feet were bare. Her toenails were painted with hot pink polish. Graham knew she liked to feel pretty, but it was getting harder and harder for her every day. It took a great deal of energy to complete the small chore of painting her toenails, and his stepfather, Quinn, had taken over the task. A few summers back, his mother had found true love in June and a lump in her breast in July. The thing she lamented was Quinn. Cancer wasn't the tragedy, finding love right before was.

She closed the sports magazine on her lap and reached for the books. Wendy was never one to follow convention, even when she was dying. Maybe there were happy endings, but too often they came too late.

"You look exhausted, Graham. Have you been working all night? Are you hungry?" She had a voice that belonged to a singer. Graham and Joel always did as she asked because she asked for so little. And how could he deny her anything now?

"I was with Ava Camden," he said. He sat down on the lounge chair next to her and waited for her reaction. The top book slipped off the pile and fell out of her grasp.

"Not our Ava Camden?" she whispered as she sat up.

"I'm sure she would object to the use of the possessive, and I can guarantee you that no one owns Ms. Camden." He sighed and picked up the book Wendy dropped.

"You want to get out of here and take a walk in the park?" he asked.

Graham didn't like the smell of the place. The medication permeated her skin, and she tried to cover up other odors with aerosol disinfectants. He felt his chest and throat constrict. Nurses and housekeepers were good at keeping things in order, clean. Quinn's jovial laugh echoed in another part of the house. Only Graham would admit that Wendy was getting worse.

It was cold for September, and a quick rain shower had just ended. The daily rain reminded Graham of his time in Jamaica. The rain would come as predictably as the sunshine.

His mother, who looked so vibrant and alive as she sat, became frail when she stood. Graham carried her like a child and placed her into a wheelchair, realizing that Wendy must have carried him like that often when he was a boy. He could think of times when he was too tired to walk or had fallen and couldn't move. His mother had been there to pick him up. He'd been there to pick up Joel.

We've got to help each other, Graham. We've only got each other. If you can't walk, then you should find someone to carry you.

It was his turn to carry her. He knelt in front of her and put her warm fuzzy socks on her feet, another shade of her favorite royal blue, and her slippers.

They left the house and crossed 10th Street. The weight of his thoughts slowed his movements. Inside Piedmont Park they traveled along a paved path next to a grassy rise. In the distance, dogs chased discs tossed by their owners. People jogged and cycled by. The last deep green before the Georgia autumn seemed dim and gray to him. Even the turning orange leaves seemed more alive than the thin form of his mother in the wheelchair. The path headed east into the blinding morning sun, and his mother turned her face to the sky. She would not live to see the New Year.

He found the spot Ava had captured in her photograph near the lake. Maybe there were ghosts under the lake and standing around the water's edge. Ava's life was so much in the shadows. She would see the New Year, but what kind of life did she have? Hiding, running, angry, and afraid.

Wendy gazed happily at the autumn morning. "Tell me about her." She leaned back and looked up at Graham upside down. She smiled, and he smiled in return.

"She doesn't like me," he started slowly.

"Ava doesn't know you, sweetheart. She'll like you eventually. Everyone does."

Graham carefully worded his impression of Ava. "She has no reason to help us, but I needed to see her. I didn't expect for her to be the way she was. Like she's not of this world."

Wendy let out a little noise that sounded like a sigh. "We need her, Graham. She's the only one who can help us get to the bottom of what really happened. Then Joel will come back to us."

"I've hired the best investigators. I'm hoping they can get to the bottom of what really happened," he said. But even as he said the words, he didn't believe it, himself.

"You're being a dreamer, Graham. A man was convicted, and that's all the courts care about. Think of the appeals over the last five years. All they and Ava's family care about is the conviction and a closed case. They don't care if it's the wrong man. They got their conviction. That's all they needed." Wendy took a labored breath.

"Mother, don't get excited. I told you I've spoken to Ava."

"Did she say she would help us?"

"Yes," he said. He needed to convince himself, too. "But I'm not sure. I wanted to tell her about you."

"Graham, I told you not to," Wendy said. Ruby embarrassment rose on her pale cheeks.

"You know what you are that she's not? Happy. You are laughter and optimism. Her photos are somber, beautiful, and deadly. She's only happy at that shelter. That's when I saw her smile."

"I wish I could meet her. I don't know her, but I trust her. She can tell Joel that she's forgiven him. That he might not be her real attacker."

"She doesn't believe that, not with the evidence they brought up against him."

"I don't know what she needs to say, but Graham, whatever it is might help bring him back."

Graham couldn't shove the terrible thought aside. *I'm sick of hearing about Joel and his conviction. Joel went to that bar and sat down next to Ava and got drunk and, for all I know, may have decided Ava was interested in him. Dear God, what if he did turn into our father? What if he did attack her? He's out of prison now. Isn't that enough?* Graham wanted to talk about Ava and things that had nothing to do with his brother. The dark color of her hair. The small perfection of her hands.

"She lives in a huge house all alone," he said. Before he knew it, he told his mother everything he knew about Ava.

Sera Camden had moved out of the mansion after Cecil died. Ava stayed in the house because she didn't mind ghosts or the solitude or the memories. Sera bought a condo near the law firm. Her life was all about work, anyway.

"How awful," Wendy said. "Ava shouldn't spend all that time alone, but the shelter sounds nice. She sounds like a good woman."

Graham asked his mother to tell him, once again, about her last visit with Joel in prison. He kept hoping there was a detail she'd forgotten, some clue to his brother's fears or plans.

She repeated the same information. Stoic, quiet Joel.

"He looked about as good as I do," she said sadly. She was

thin and almost translucent in her paleness. All of her hair was gone. She wore a blue knit cap.

"Then he must have looked beautiful."

Graham bent down and placed a kiss on her check. She was cold, so he turned to take her back home. Unfortunately, Joel never fought the conviction. He accepted his fate as if he must be guilty.

If I find him, I'll move him to Jamaica, Graham thought. Graham loved the island as a young man in the construction business. The Caribbean sun had darkened his fair skin. Often the lone white guy on the construction teams, he was accustomed to being the minority—in the black neighborhoods of Atlanta's southside and among the black administrations and business elite of the city.

When the prosecution initially brought hate-crime charges against Joel, it had been one of the more painful moments for Graham. Was that how Ava felt after the attack, under the media's scrutiny? A black woman who had been victimized because of her race? The charge was dropped—too hard to prove but interesting for the media.

Cecil Camden made sure he told the media that the city would not stand for any more crimes that went unpunished because of race. Justice would prevail for his daughter. Was Joel's prosecution supposed to right a century of wrong? Maybe an eternity of injustice.

He looked at his hands, clean and cold. There was no justice for anyone.

Graham remembered the last time he saw his brother. He went through registration, security, and finally moved to a line of waiting to enter in a large room that resembled a school cafeteria. The tables were filled with prisoners waiting to see their families. When the doors opened, Graham felt the air change, wives and children rushed forward with smiles.

"I think you'll have a chance at parole next year," was the only comfort Graham could provide. "I'm working on that. I promise you. Three years early on a ten-year sentence. I think my lawyers can swing it."

Joel only responded with, "I'm a dead man. Whenever I walk out of here. Everyone hates me." He'd wiped his hands over his face.

We all have scars.

Joel's hands seemed empty when he didn't have a football in them. They were strong hands, the hands of a man who knew how to work. He could fix a motorcycle or overturn soil with his bare hands. It was the only thing they shared in common as children. A love of the dirt.

Before their father drank himself to death, they lived in a little one bedroom apartment near a tiny empty lot where the community had created a garden. Mom's imagination turned it into a hidden kingdom. She would send the boys into the community garden and tell them to search for pirate treasure, which, of course, could only be found by pulling up weeds.

They never fit in at schools. They were poorer than even the poorest of kids. The only thing that saved them was being big and tall and not afraid of a fight. That, and a love of books, education. Hard work. Both of them had worked to make Mom proud, to get out of poverty, to be Somebody. But in one horrible might, that dream was taken not just from Joel, but from Graham and their mother, too. Where was the justice in that?

Ava, with her big empty house and all the money in the world, grew up with few friends. Where was the justice in that? Why did he think he could fix anything if everything was broken?

Graham adjusted his mother's feet on her wheelchair's footrests and followed the path with the most shade. Wendy had too late found security and love. Graham would take her back to her house. He figured where the dying lived were the fewest ghosts.

Chapter 17

THERE WERE A few parking spaces behind The Light House. When Ava opened the door at 4:01 p.m., Graham Sapphire and another man stood at the back of a pickup truck unloading boxes. Ava checked in the other volunteers and propped open the door.

"What's all this?" she asked.

Graham had a baseball cap on. The "A" for Atlanta Braves looked like the emblem of a superhero on him. He pulled off the cap, and the other man did the same.

"This is my mother's nurse, Elliot Strickland. He's on loan from Mom."

Elliot looked like he could lift the truck they drove. But he shook her hand carefully. "Pleasure to meet you, Ms. Camden."

Ava returned the sentiment to the man. He went back to unloading the truck like he'd been briefed on the delicate situation he was being brought into. "Graham . . ." she started.

He interrupted her. "Towels, soaps, shampoo." Did they have a fragile truce? She ruined that when she'd threatened him with the knife.

I am sorry. I'm not insane. I'm a little lost.

"Thank you," she said, because he wouldn't accept her apology. She was thankful for the supplies. She ran her hand along the perfectly sealed edge of one of the boxes. "This is amazing." They'd never received donations in even numbers before. They were glad for broken boxes and leftovers. New supplies specifically meant for the shelter were a true gift.

Graham ignored her thanks and kept unloading. Ava snapped herself back to reality. This much stuff was more than they would need for six weeks. She picked up a box and headed inside. The two men followed her.

The storage room was overflowing with mismatched items and boxes of different sizes. Food and toiletries and cleaning supplies. When Ava wasn't there for a few days, order fell right back into chaos.

Graham walked in behind her. "Elliot can get this straightened out while we bring the rest of the boxes."

Ava paused. This was her order to create. Graham sensed her hesitation. "He's got it. If you don't like it, you can fix it after he leaves."

The last bit of heat warmed the day before the sun went down. After five trips to Graham's truck, Ava felt a trickle of sweat going down her back. Lance and the rest of the staff usually prevented her from doing the heavy lifting. But it felt good.

She'd always been physically strong. Her daddy hadn't raised her and Nadine to be weak. While other kids played video games, she and Nadine planted gardens. She could shovel and dig and tell when the soil was right for planting tomatoes. They built a tree house. Cecil Camden drew the plans, and the girls learned to hammer and calculate the lengths of wood that could support their weight. By the time Nadine was ten and Ava eight, their parents were too busy building a legal empire to make the girls dig, but they enjoyed digging by that time. Nadine still planted her own tomatoes and carrots and herbs. Ava still fixed up the tree house when planks needed mending.

Nights in the shelter involved paper work more than heavy lifting, and Ava had forgotten the joy of doing a task that had an end. Much of her life was filled with intangibles. Anger, hate, memory. Those things had no end. Move, stack, count boxes. These things could be done and finished.

Graham and Ava went back outside, where the alley was quiet and the sky faded to purple. He retrieved a bottle of water from the front seat and took a swig. He wore a white t-shirt that clung to his triceps, down his hard chest and flat stomach. The shirt became slightly translucent with his perspiration. She saw the outline of a bandage where she cut him. Or had he cut himself? His jeans sat low on his hips, only being loose at the waist. Her eyes fell to his thighs and down to his work boots. She suddenly felt thirsty. In her mind, she kept apologizing, but sorry wasn't the right word for how she was feeling.

When their eyes met, he looked embarrassed, as though she'd been judging him. Graham took another swig of water from the bottle he carried and gently held it out to her.

"You need some water?"

She wanted to say no. She wanted to say she didn't need a drink. She wanted to explain that she had not been judging him for his clothes or his work boots. He wouldn't believe her if she said the dirt on his boots made her trust him.

"Sure." She accepted the bottle against her better judgment and took a small sip. She was thirsty and could taste the salt from his lips on the mouth of the bottle. Ava quickly recapped the water and handed it back toward him.

"How are you feeling today?" he asked. "Better, I hope."

"Yes and no. Yes, about the allergic reaction, but I'm not feeling better about what I did to you."

"I don't want to talk about that. That's nothing. It's already forgotten."

She tried to catch his eyes while he avoided hers. Ava continued speaking, hoping to catch him with her words. "All that medicine makes me feel a little shaky for a while, but it's gone now. I appreciate you staying with me at the hospital. I should've called my mother. The whole thing put you in an awkward position, and I apologize."

"I don't want you to apologize to me anymore. Clean slate, starting today. I like your company better than compiling annual reports and reviewing marketing strategies." He locked and closed the truck door as he spoke and then went to the back and closed the truck bed.

"Graham? The other staff members, they don't know about the shelter being closed down. Even my friend Lance. I haven't told any of them yet."

"Okay. I understand."

"Well, that makes one of us. Because I don't understand. And before I start in on another Mommy-Dearest tirade, I better get back to work. I'm usually pretty tied up until ten o'clock, then I work in the office. Do you want to come back? How did you want to do this?"

"Is it okay if I stay and help out? Elliot likes to cook, and quite honestly, if you put him to work, he can clean and cut hair, too. I can review your financials for the shelter if you want. Expenses, donations. I can catalog liabilities or draft business requirements to keep this place open. You'll need to consider the cost of buying the building out-right. If that isn't an option, I have a broker who can find other locations if you have to move."

"I wasn't thinking about the shelter. I thought you wanted to talk about your brother."

He was silent for so long that she grew worried. Ava watched his expression darken more with each second. Finally he said, "My brother has chosen to disappear. To walk away from me and our mother, even though he knows that I would have protected him, taken care of him, and that she desperately wants to see him. He doesn't want to talk to me or her. I've never called him selfish in my life, but right now I don't know how I feel about fighting for someone who's walked away from the only people who've stood behind him the last seven years."

"I am willing to help you," she said, and he exhaled a pent-up breath. "The shelter is everything in the entire world to me, but I can't sleep or eat or breathe until I finish this thing with your brother. I'm willing to forgive him—at least, to say the words—which is something I never thought I'd hear myself doing—if you think that will help bring him out of hiding. I'm hoping it might even help me. I need you to specify exactly what you want from me."

Graham ran his hands through his hair. "I don't know," he sighed. "I have the case files. All of them. I have those pictures. I honestly don't know what else I need. I'm looking for a missing piece."

"You want me to help you, but you don't know what to believe yourself. Make me believe that he's innocent, Graham. You don't sound as sure, anymore."

"What you told me about the bar worries me. Even though the only thing I fault him for is getting drunk. Just hearing you describe how it happened . . . I'm being honest with you."

She sighed, "I'm a terrible person. I want Joel to be guilty, Graham. You don't realize what you are suggesting." She looked up at him not realizing that by doing so she was undoing him, her black eyes luminous in the shadowy night. "I can try to forgive him, but I can't say he didn't do it. If Joel didn't attack me, then who did?"

Chapter 18

PROVING HIS BROTHER innocent had always been one side of the coin, along with proving someone else had attacked Ava. Now that he was part of her life, caring about her, the idea that her real attacker was still out there twisted his gut. As those thoughts went through his mind, he felt Ava's fear increase. Her breath changed. Her eyes stopped connecting with his and focused on distant points.

Graham stepped close to her and grabbed her hand.

"I'm the one who is sorry about last night. I shouldn't have grabbed the knife. I shouldn't have scared you the way I did. I'm going to talk to Martin Brown first. Then everyone else I can find. See if anyone can think of anything. And let's find that bartender."

Ava squeezed his hand as he spoke. She didn't know that she held onto him like a lifeline. Graham didn't want to get used to the feeling of her hand in his.

"She was interviewed by the detectives," Ava said. "Her name will be in the case files."

The restaurant had closed the year after the attack, shut down by the franchise owner after Cecil Camden sued for millions on Ava's behalf. Under pressure from Cecil, the landlord had torn out the front and side façade of the building, removing the scene of the attack right down to the concrete on which Ava had bled.

She pulled her hand away from Graham's. "I only want the truth. Do you believe that?"

He nodded.

"I'm going with you to see Martin Brown. You only want to hear one specific thing, that Joel didn't do it. I want to hear what Martin has to say. Thank him for his help that night. If you go in your way, you'll never get what you want. We'll go to Martin together. We'll look through the files and find the name of the bartender. We can talk to her if you want. Together."

"I don't think you should go."

"No. These are my scars. We do this together or not at all."

"Ava, you need to stay in the background."

"Not become a target, you mean. If you really believe Joel is innocent, then the man who cut me might—"

"I'm trying not to scare you, and I swear to you I'm not trying to keep you from getting the answers you want. I don't think you should be with me when I start asking questions about this case around Atlanta."

"I'm not asking questions. I'm only thanking people for their help all those years ago. Have you ever tried to contact any of the witnesses? Did you ever try to talk to anyone during the trial? If you confront people now, it will be dangerous for me whether I'm along for the questions or not. Remember how you came into the shelter? You didn't come up to me and say, 'I'm Joel's brother.' You walked in, watched, waited. We need to be careful. See how people react."

"I've never personally contacted Martin or anyone else related to the trial. My attorneys have. My investigators. I let the professionals do their job. Until you. Now it's personal in a whole new way."

Graham felt a small jolt of satisfaction when she inhaled sharply at his words. Ava wore her hair down at the art gallery, but at the shelter she pulled it back. She stood straight, and everything about her was unguarded. Her sense of wonder at the boxes of supplies, her fear about the truth, even her trust in him. She leaned slightly toward him, and he inhaled her scent. She used some plain soap that lacked perfume. Here at the shelter she was without guise.

"I don't want you to get hurt," she said. Her eyes flickered to the hidden bandage. "Again."

"I want to do this alone, Ava. I want you to trust me."

"I don't know. That's what the nurse in the hospital said about you. I *must* trust you. I'm not sure if it was an order or the truth."

Graham smiled. It was the first real smile Ava had seen of his. "Pearl said that? Your nurse offered me half her dinner. Nice lady. She owes me a home-cooked Jamaican meal." He looked at the sky. The city lights were beginning to turn on. The moon was already up in the purple sky. "Look, Ava, can we worry about the shelter tonight and not Joel? I'll help Elliot in the stock room and let you get back to work. Later, you can show me your financials for the running of this place."

They found Elliot organizing the supplies alphabetically, and Ava gave a little nod of approval.

"I'll be in my office getting a few of the records together."

Graham had already decided he'd find out the truth without her.

SERA CAMDEN WORE a brown tweed suit contrasted with dangerously high stilettos. She stood in Ava's office with two other members of the Camden Foundation board of directors. The three extra people could hardly fit in the same space of the office at the shelter. They were used to their big law firm offices. They huddled together, whispering, but stopped when Ava walked into the room. Sera shook her daughter's hand. Ava noticed the dry coldness of her mother's palm and thought the greeting was a little too formal, even for her mother.

Though dark and filled with the scent of lemon cleaner, her office at the shelter was immaculate. Sunday night at the shelter was not usually the place she ran into the board members. They were still starched and clean from church.

"I know you've had a trying couple of days now that Joel Sapphire is out of jail. We cannot imagine the additional stress that this has caused you, but we have good news. This will keep your mind off of him," Sera said. Her smile had gone from a natural grin that lit up her eyes to a stiff version of its former self. Her mother was no more comfortable bringing up Joel than Ava was hearing about him.

One of the board members cleared his throat. "We've been impressed with the growth and direction you've taken with the men's shelter over the last several years, and it is with that spirit that the Camden Foundation would like to change the scope of The Light House. We plan to consolidate services with another shelter in Atlanta."

Ava felt her heart turn over in her chest. This was the official story. That's why Mother had brought the board members. They knew Ava wanted to do more than provide beds, meals, and haircuts. These men needed literacy classes, technical training, transition to permanent housing, and real world skills to help them get off the streets.

"That's great, Mother. I have a list of ideas that I've been trying to get approved by the board for years. These men can really benefit—"

"Not only men, Ava," Sera continued. "We are closing down this program in forty-five days and reallocating our funding to Peachtree Missions. Men, women, and families. Parents with children or single mothers and single fathers who are not eligible to stay in other shelters. Right now in Atlanta there are dozens of shelters for men, a handful for women, and only a couple that cater to homeless families that want to stay together. There is a need in our community, and the Camden Foundation is always looking toward the future. Peachtree Missions is the future."

"Shouldn't we keep this shelter open to continue to meet the need in the community here?"

"The city wants this location back. There have been concerns about the impact your tenants have on the surrounding neighborhood. This part of town is going through a renaissance. A homeless shelter is no longer wanted here. This isn't me. It's the city. We have to determine how the Camden Foundation's community effort will look going forward."

"I can get started on a strategic plan tomorrow."

Sera turned away. The other two board members exchanged uncomfortable looks. Ava stared at her mother's back and wished she'd get to the point. There wasn't a view from the 44th floor, so her mother looked at the extra supplies stacked on the floor. Everything was beneath her at the law firm. Her view of the world was always from above, but at The Light House Sera was stuck on the ground.

"We plan to hire a person to run the new program."

"Are you firing me?" Ava asked. "You can't fire me when I work for free. The Camden Foundation bears my family's name, and you have no right to replace me." She wanted to say more, but the words she needed to say refused to come out of her mouth.

Sera turned. "This is my decision. Both you and this shelter have been stagnating for years. We need a public face for fundraising efforts, and that's not something you are willing to do. We need to expand the scope of our outreach program, but I could see you paling at the idea of housing women and children, the two groups of people most in need of our services. It is selfish of you not to want to improve this shelter, because this is where you feel comfortable. Eventually, we all have to step out of our skin and try something new. We want you to be involved every step of the way, but you aren't ready to stand in front of a camera and give a press conference or host a charity ball. When you are ready, we can rethink your involvement, but for now, you've got six weeks to shut down this shelter and decide what you want to do next."

Ava had gotten only two hours of sleep the night before, and her eyes were dry and stinging. Camden's did not cry. She had heard her mother weeping in the hospital, but she never saw her cry.

"I understand completely, Mrs. Camden," Ava said. "Marketing and PR supersede the need for a well-run program."

"Ava, there are people trained to run the programs we are trying to develop. Men and woman with degrees in social work, urban studies, and law. You said yourself you were never a lawyer, so these are skills you don't have. You fell into this position by happenstance. You had no interest in working with the homeless until you were attacked. Camden, Franks, & Rose is willing to be a significant contributor to this new endeavor. You have one hundred beds. They'll put in two hundred more beds at Peachtree Missions. The firm is also willing to offer you an associate level position as an attorney in the law firm in their new charitable planning division. This is an opportunity for you to go back to a real job."

"This job is real. I can put my hands in someone else's hands. I can touch the food. I know that Peachtree Missions has more services, and we partner with them all the time. You don't have to shut this place down. And I'd rather live on the streets than work for your law firm. The day I agree to work at Camden, Franks, & Rose is the day I decide I've given up on life. Do you want me to turn out like dad?"

Ava stopped the other words before they came out of her mouth.

I watched him die. He didn't love any of us enough to keep living. Not you, not Nadine, not me. The only thing he loved was work. If I go back to work with you, daddy's ghost will be there. Not worth the money. Not worth power. Mother, I don't want to hate you like I hate him.

"It may look like it to you, Mother, but I haven't given up yet."

Sera sighed, "You've got forty-five days to get everything in order with this shelter before we close it down. I'm sorry about this Ava, truly I am, but I don't think you are ready. Closing down The Light House is the best thing for this community, and I think the change will be a good thing for you, too."

"What about Lance Bertram? He's worked here since day one. He's got as much invested in this shelter as I do."

"He'll be offered a job at Peachtree Missions, if he wants one."

"But not me."

"No, not you."

They filed out of her office with mumbled goodbyes. Ava spun around in her chair and looked at the clock. Time had been slipping away from her all day. They could and would take the shelter away from her. What else did she have to lose after that?

A knock on the door drew her attention, and Graham stood in the doorway.

Eight weeks, maybe less. He'll be gone, too.

I'll help you with the shelter.

"You okay?" he asked.

I'm fine.

"How come your mother didn't get a restraining order against me?"

Ava looked up and tried not to stare. She didn't often have a tall, overly handsome man leaning into her office with a somber impression on his face. Graham had one hand casually on the top of the door frame. A door frame she wouldn't be able to reach even with the help of a ladder.

"I spoke to my friend, Brad Vargas. He's a police officer, and he's probably watching you. You know how some people have an angel on one shoulder and a devil on the other? That's Brad."

"Which one is he? Angel or devil?"

"I don't know yet."

"Then you won't be disappointed when you find out." Graham stepped forward. "Are you hungry? You haven't missed dinner yet. Do you want to eat with me?"

She sensed he was prepared for her rejection like it didn't matter. He was braced for her to say no.

"I'd love to eat, say hi to Lance, and see who's in the shelter tonight."

She stood and walked over to him, but Graham didn't move out of the doorway. She was glad he didn't back away. She was glad his voice filled the quiet of the room.

"Eat with us, see who you need to see, and then go home, Ava. I'm asking you to do a favor for me. Don't drive around Atlanta. Go to your house and your bed. Go to sleep. You need rest. I don't think you've had any sleep since I've met you. I'll help Lance here at the shelter. Elliot and I will fill in wherever you would have."

She shook her head. "I can't go home. I need to be here. Otherwise, I'll do what I shouldn't do."

"What's that?" he asked. He could take away her cold, and he could take away her fear.

"I'll follow the sirens. Tonight would be the first night that I don't, and I'd rather stay here. I don't want to go home.

I can't sleep."

"Neither can I, Ava. I don't sleep. Do you know why?"

The feeling in her chest she'd first called anger and later fear was something else. She could smell the sweetness of his sweat. Every part of him had a scent.

She wasn't going to be afraid of anything anymore. The past. The sunlight. Closing the doors on the shelter. Ava put a hand on Graham's chest. She thought it would make him take a step back, but he stayed in the doorway.

She blinked slowly and imagined Graham moving the hair away from her face and leaning down to kiss her. Her mouth opened, and her eyes moved to his lips.

What happens in fairy tales? Do you need a kiss to wake up or a kiss to go to sleep?

Ava knew for certain that if she kissed Graham Sapphire, he would kiss her back. Instead of leaning up to his mouth, she traced a finger along his shirt. Underneath was his new scar.

"It would be easier if we both hated each other. Scars are a special kind of shield. You are beautiful, Graham. It's all that kindness in you. I wish I had some. You take care of your brother, your mom, and now me. How do you do it?"

She would have pulled her hand away, but he covered her hand with his and held it fast to his chest.

"I wasn't very kind last night when I grabbed your hand while I cut myself. I shouldn't have done it. You see, I want a lot of things, Ava. I want things that would make you blush. These are things I cannot have. Do you hear me? I'm not what you think I am. You mistake my restraint for kindness, and you're wrong. I don't want you to go home alone either."

She couldn't focus on his words when his heart beat strongly against her palm. His heart beat was strong enough to keep them both alive.

Please, God. Don't let him be kind to me.

"If it isn't kindness, that's fine with me. I'll thank you for your restraint. You are right. I should try to sleep. Lance can tell you where the files are."

She pulled her hand away from his chest.

He whispered, "I should walk away from you right now because of what you did with that knife. When Joel was arrested, I was devastated. I spent day and night trying to get him released. Then he was convicted, and I spent years orchestrating appeals and retrials without success. Do you know how many women offered themselves to me during those years? Every woman I've met the past seven years has wanted me to hurt them. They whispered in my ears about handcuffs and ropes and whips. They all thought it would be fun to pretend to be hurt. Sapphire men can be dangerous. They couldn't get to my brother, even though he developed quite a fan following in prison. The rest wanted to sleep with the brother of a criminal. They wanted me to have sex with them, but with special requests. Some of them asked me to hold them by their throats. Others wanted me to slap them. One in particular wanted me to take a knife to her skin as I undressed her. These were probably even some of your rich society friends. That's not me. I can't do that. Is that what you want from me, Ava?"

"No."

He relaxed the way he braced his body in the doorway. "I could never hurt you. There is good in this world, and you are one of those good things, Ava. I'll never forget the person who offered me a place to sleep and a bowl of food when she thought I didn't have anything. These men won't forget you if you go home early tonight. If you get scared, call me. If you are too scared to call me, think of me."

Graham touched her face. Ava moistened her lips with her tongue. He followed the gesture intently.

I'm thirsty.

"Ava, I wrote to you all those years, because I thought you might listen even though we had nothing in common. Not our past, not our future. I thought you would understand my anger and confusion. You never responded, and I still felt better talking to you than anyone else in the world. If you learn to sleep, maybe I will, too."

Sleep seemed like a dream. She would go home. Her home was another void, another place for her to hide. The idea of a good night's sleep was a new challenge. She needed to be normal for her nieces. Sleep was one of those normal things. Eyes closed at night and being awake during the daylight. If she couldn't sleep, maybe she could lie down and imagine her new future. After seven years of wakefulness and the heat of his chest still warm on her hand, she wasn't afraid of sleep. Ava was afraid of finding Graham only in her dreams.

Chapter 19

SHE TRIED TO sleep but failed. Ava wished she could say that her bad nights started dark and rainy and enveloped in fog, but the sky was clear and starry. No sirens echoed. The moon hung large and orange near the horizon. For the first time in seven years, a different Sapphire was on her mind.

Graham would try to solve the past without her help. To protect her.

But it was her past, too. Her scars. And his life in danger, too.

Ava gathered her coat and headed to the door. 12:01 a.m. Too many hours until dawn. She held her coat close around her body and pulled on the hood even though there was no wind and no rain. In the cold, the scent of pine trees grew stronger. They were her evergreen guardians. She never felt afraid on the dark streets. This had been Ava's favorite hour. Sweet midnight.

Graham had said get sleep, but Ava would have to learn how after all the questions were answered. She looked at the pictures of her and Joel a dozen times. She wrote down a new narrative of the night she was attacked. She tried to remember as many small details as she could.

A tattoo on the bartender's wrist read, "Today is always here. Tomorrow never."

The person who attacked me wore bells. Bells are a warning sound.

I heard the whispered words, "She'll never leave me after she sees your face."

Ava drove down Peachtree Street then down side streets into a shopping district several blocks from the shelter. In the hours after midnight, this area was empty. The silence helped keep her sane.

She wasted time idly looking in the backlit store windows.

She walked past a headless mannequin in an ivory dress. The strapless gown clung to the gaunt frame of the model, and she could tell that the fabric was a heavy silk. Ava's head was a perfect match for the mannequin's missing one.

I would trade places with you if I could.

Her own reflection seemed more at home on the lifeless twin.

Her hand drifted upward towards the glass. But she pulled it back. Only the insane made friends with mannequins. She wasn't insane. She wasn't insane. She only needed sleep.

Ava wore a dark gray coat. It was knee length and hooded so that she could hide inside it. She pulled the hood up and continued her slow circle, pausing at a children's boutique. There were tiaras perfect for Lydia and Lexi. Maybe it was good to pretend you were a princess. She noticed the sound of footsteps approaching.

She didn't look back. Her instincts told her it was better not to turn, not to see the dangers that could approach her in the night. She felt a presence following her. She imagined the stunning pain of a blow to the back of her head and an icy hand descending over her throat. It can't happen again. She wouldn't let it.

She turned toward the sound of the footsteps. A man stopped several stores away at the same window she had seen the headless mannequin. Maybe he wasn't following her. She had become good at hiding. For the first time in a long time, she was afraid.

She was half a mile from her car, in a "nice" part of the city. Ava had been careful. She turned back, and the man was gone. Not once in all these years had she been followed.

She hurried back in the direction of her car. If she ran she could make it there faster. She turned and sprinted though the park in the middle of the small shopping center. Her only hindrance was the coat. As she ran, the hood fell away from her face. The cold air went into her lungs in painful breaths.

Footsteps followed her again. She hadn't gotten a look at the man pursuing her. She didn't want to look back, to let him gain on her.

She curled off into a landscaped border. Pine needles covered the cold ground, making her path slick and dangerous. She scrambled between the thicket of shrubs and branches.

She wouldn't let him catch her.

The harder she ran, the more piercingly cold the air became. Each breath sliced into her lungs like the serrated edges of a knife. But she had to move faster. She heard faster steps behind her. Gaining on her as she ran. Terror seized her. She darted toward the parking lot. The air was full of pine and decaying wood. She heard a dog bark in the distance.

She was close to her car. In a minute, if she pushed it, she would be on the pavement of the lot and moving faster. She dodged right then left to avoid falling. Angry roots pulled from the earth like fingers. Footsteps sounded behind her. And laughter.

She tripped and fell. A hand grabbed her right foot. She screamed. She kicked. She fought. Her shoe came off.

I'll save myself.

No one will hurt me again.

Everything became very quiet. Ava closed her eyes. She was certain she felt the familiar taste of blood in her mouth, running down her face. When she opened her eyes, the park was empty. The trees were illuminated by street lights. Her foot was caught in the tangle of a kudzu vine. She blinked and breathed and blinked again. She was alone. No one was following her. No one was there.

Chapter 20

GRAHAM TOOK IN a deep breath. The air was cool, crisp, and clean. He felt frustrated at the stillness of the night while his mind raged. A few bright stars could be seen through the glow of the Atlanta city lights. He'd never made a wish in his life. Why would he start now? A man with thoughts about the only woman he couldn't have didn't deserve wishes. He felt the imprint of Ava's hand on his chest from earlier that night.

Should I move these boxes?

There are the two available warehouses in the five block square radius from here.

I found the bartender's name. I called Martin Brown.

The indirect questions were dangerous.

Are you lonely without me?

Are you sleeping? Are you dreaming about me?

He wanted to know the answers to the questions.

Elliot had gone home hours earlier to check on Quinn and Wendy. Graham paced in front of the sad little building that housed the shelter.

There were people milling about who had no intention of going inside. A few women were scattered along the block. They walked up to men in hopes of taking money from them in exchange for their bodies. On another corner, men exchanged discreet handshakes without slowing their stride.

"Hey," a lady called out to him from down the street. Graham couldn't tell if she was sixty years old or twenty. Her stringy blond hair had gone brown and weathered like her face. Her jawline was pronounced because so many of her teeth were missing. Her short skirt revealed skeletal legs. This skin of her body had nothing to cling to.

Graham tensed as she moved closer. During one of their poorest years, Mom had scratched together enough to take the three of them to a diner one night for an all-you-could-eat deal. They'd stuffed themselves and slipped everything they could carry into their pockets and her purse. Walking home, a man stopped them and said something to her.

Graham didn't hear the words, but his mother tensed, which frightened him. She'd taken beatings from Dad until Graham was nine, when Graham became the object of his attacks, too. It took a lot to scare her. She tensed, and she paused. He was afraid she might leave them to go with the man, but she started walking. Faster, more determined.

That was the moment she decided the three of them would fight back.

"Everybody and everything has been hard on us, but now we are going to be the ones to make it hard for ourselves. I'm telling you that if you don't ever want to be hit or hungry again, we can make it, but it is going to be rough. Studying is hard, staying out of trouble is hard. I don't only mean police, but I mean girls, too. They bring trouble. Friends bring trouble."

That's when Graham started reading books on how to win at dice, win at cards, and later win in business. That was when Joel started running and doing push-ups and pull-ups and turning himself into something other than the scrawny picked-on kid he'd been. Graham had a natural bulk, where Joel was lean.

"Hey," the lady said again. It was trouble calling.

He nodded at her and kept pacing.

"I'm talking to you. Don't you like what you see?"

"I'm looking for a different type, no hard feelings."

"I've got a friend who can help you."

"No, thanks."

Great, a full service prostitution ring. He had to admire the business mindedness of her offer. He wished he had some money in his pockets to give her for the trouble, but Graham knew enough about the streets to travel empty handed. No wallet, no credit cards. That'd be inviting trouble in this part of town, and trouble already followed him in the daylight. No reason to tempt the night.

A car pulled up in front of Graham, blocking the road. The tires screeched as it stopped. Three guys jumped out before the car stopped rolling.

Graham tensed when all their eyes turned directly on him.

"Betty, go down the street and don't come back," one of the guys ordered. He was calm and polite, as if he were directing traffic. They all wore brand new sneakers, jeans tailored to fit, and white t-shirts. None of them wore coats. Whatever business they had would be handled quickly, and they'd be back in the warmth of their car.

"He's not bothering me," the lady shouted. She stumbled a bit but moved away like they said.

"Ice, you the one looking for your brother?"

Graham never got to answer as the first guy slammed a fist into his face. The knuckles burst across his temples, but he recovered quickly and got in two quick punches of his own. The second guy jumped on him, and they landed in a heap on the ground.

He felt a kick to his side, and the other guy pounded his ribs. He grabbed a foot before another strike, and one of the thugs fell to the pavement. Suddenly there were shouts, and he felt more blows to his body than he could withstand. They were leaving his face alone, but his kidneys, ribs, and his insides were on fire. They were trying to kill him.

Suddenly everything went quiet. He slowly opened his eyes, but the world was listing back and forth like a ship in a storm. He thought he saw Ava coming toward him like a shadow. Half the residents from her shelter spilled onto the street. Why didn't he hear sirens?

She turned to the men who followed her. "Get back inside." She pointed to Lance, "It's lockdown. Now. Anyone who is still outside in two minutes, stays outside all night. You boys know I'm careful about time."

Lance ushered the men inside. Someone complained, "We can't leave her out there."

Same thing Graham was thinking. He was dreaming, because not only was she staying outside alone, but she was walking slowly towards him, keeping her eyes on the four men the whole time.

She had no gun. She had no baseball bat. She didn't even have a phone.

"Leave him alone," Ava said.

"What? You're kidding right?" Two of the guys started laughing.

"I mean it. He came into my shelter. That means he's under my protection. Get away from him," she ordered.

The guys shook their heads, and Ava smiled. It was not the smile of a happy person.

The leader lifted up his shirt and showed a gun tucked into his pants.

"You don't even know what you're doing, Nightingale. We did this for you."

Sirens sounded in the distance. She very carefully stepped forward under the streetlight and tucked her hair behind her ears and away from her face so she could see Graham. There must have been blood on his temple from the first blow to his face. Her hands went to that spot as she crouched down and looked up at the looming figures.

"You know I can't let anyone be hurt on my watch."

"I'm fine," Graham mumbled. "Go back inside."

She stood back up and stepped between him and the other men.

Maybe she really wanted to die.

One of the guys tossed up his hands as if she'd closed down a party that was just starting to be fun. "We're doing you a favor. You going to pick him over us?"

"He came into the shelter. The sign inside the door says, 'We protect all who enter here.' All. That even means you if you ever needed a place to stay."

"You are crazy. I never thought so until this."

"I never thought you guys were bullies who ganged up on people until this."

Sirens sounded again, and Ava smiled again. They hurried to their car and drove off. The spectators sauntered back to their street corners. Another night, another street fight.

Graham felt Ava's hand slip inside his shirt to inspect the damage. There was his burn mark on the right side of his waist. Before she could get a better look, Graham grabbed his shirt and pulled it down. His chest burned, and his lungs felt like he was breathing firewater.

The old prostitute shuffled near to inspect Graham.

"I wanted to know if he thought I was pretty," the woman mumbled and then walked down the street.

"Lance?" Ava called. Her friend was at the door keeping the men from her shelter inside. He ran over when she called his name.

"Ava, you've got to stop doing stuff like that," he said. "That's the kind of thing that makes your mother mad."

Ava ran her hand along Graham's ribs. It was a wonder they weren't broken. *He'll get killed trying to help me.* It was time to make a decision. "She's shutting us down anyway. But until those doors are closed for good, I own this street."

"What?" Lance asked.

"No more shelter. This is it. We've got a little over a month. That's why Graham's been looking at the financials. I should have mentioned he's not a volunteer from the foundation. He's trying to figure out what I can do to save this place. And his last name is Sapphire. Grab his other shoulder so we can get him up."

She was always protecting people.

Graham tried to shrug them off, but he didn't have the strength. "Why'd you let her come out alone, Lance?" Graham trailed off.

"I don't *let* Ms. Camden anything. She calls the shots," Lance said. "And, Ava. I knew he was a Sapphire. He told me."

She crouched at Graham's side and threw his arm over her shoulder. Lance did the same on the other side. Must have been something they did regularly. They moved Graham to a kneeling position without exchanging any words.

"I think I'm going to be sick," Graham whispered.

"You better do that out here before we get you up," Ava said.

"Get away. I'm okay." He crawled towards the curb and storm drain. The contents of his stomach fell out of him without effort. He felt broken everywhere.

Ava and Lance stayed at his side. It'd been a long time since Graham had anyone to lean on.

"Do you have someone who might be worried about you? Is there someone we should call?" Ava asked.

"No. I have no one. And I'm not going back inside the shelter. No need to stir up the residents."

"It's the shelter or I call an ambulance. I'm sure your friend Pearl will be unhappy to see you like this."

"I've taken worse beatings than this. I know when my ribs are broken. I'm okay."

"Shelter it is," Ava ordered even though they were already halfway to the door.

"But I don't understand. Were you trying to get yourself killed? You see four guys jump me, and you rush right into the middle of it?"

"They know I run the shelter. I mean business. And it appeared they knew you."

"I don't know. 'Ice' was my nickname back in high school, but that was years ago. Funny nickname for a white guy in an all-black school. If they've been causing trouble around here, why didn't you call the police?"

Lance stopped to lock the door and shook his head at Ava. She shouldered Graham's weight alone as they continued down the hallway. She led him to her office and perched him on her desk.

She rummaged through her desk and pulled out a first aid kit.

They protect all who enter here. Even me.

He leaned back and closed his eyes hearing sirens again, not sure if they were on the street, coming for him, or in his mind.

"Do you still want to die, Ava? You shouldn't have come out for me like that. Why didn't you call the police?"

"Graham, you don't understand. That *was* the police."

Chapter 21

SHE'D BEEN FOLLOWING sirens for seven years, and Ava knew almost everyone on the police force. The altercation with the police was no accident, but they hadn't expected her to show up or defend Graham.

Ava grabbed a first aid kit from the shelf and moved between his legs as he sat on her desk. She helped him pull the t-shirt from his body. The wound on his collarbone had reopened. She cleaned that one first. She felt responsible as it shed new blood. He gave a sharp inhale when she wiped the area with alcohol. Her face was so close to his, his breath danced across her forehead.

The only mark on his face was a cut on his temple. She gingerly reached up to wipe it clean. In doing so, she brought her body up against him. He slowed his breathing on purpose as though he'd lost his breath. She felt his eyes on every movement she made.

"Did you know those guys? Were they really the police?" Graham asked.

She nodded. "Off-duty. Someone must have told them you were here."

"I've only ever been hit by my father. I made excuses as a boy, feeling like the beatings were my fault. I could prevent them if I tried. Or I could take them in the place of someone else I loved. Is that crazy? He's been dead twenty years, and when those guys jumped me, I felt my father's hands on me. It's like no one can hurt me but him."

"That's how I feel about your brother. In a way, I've felt invincible, until tonight. Tonight I was scared."

"Ava, look at me." She stood close, but her eyes were distant. "Why'd you come back to the shelter?"

"I couldn't sleep. I did some prowling nearby. And then . . . I thought a man was following me." She took a labored breath.

He grasped her shoulders. "What?"

"My imagination! No one was there. But I was so spooked. I had to get back to the shelter where it is safe, and by the time I got here, the men were running out to see a fight in the street. They wanted to see what was happening."

He gently tilted her face back so he could look at her. Heat emanated from her, and she belatedly realized that she was still wearing her coat. "I was waiting for you. Hoping you'd come back." Even though he was the one who was hurt, Graham opened the buttons of her heavy coat. She didn't resist his help. "Are you sure you're all right? You hurt your face."

She nodded. "I've already cleaned up my scratches. I fell down. I feel so stupid. No one was chasing me. Let me see you." She stepped back between his legs. She ordered him to lift up his arms. His sides had bruises and abrasions. "You need ice packs, and I can bandage your chest. You're sure nothing is broken?"

"I'm sure. That's a different kind of pain. I don't need anything. I'm fine. Isn't that your line? 'I had an accident, but now I'm fine.' But you're the one shaking. Come here."

"I don't like to see people being hurt. The guys here know this shelter is a safe zone. No fighting. If they fight they have to leave. I don't make any exceptions."

It was the first time she got to look at his face leisurely. The small cut at his temple would not leave a permanent mark, but only this man could bear a scar and still be called beautiful.

She wasn't crying, and she hadn't thought of herself as a woman who frightened easily. She courted dangerous hours and places every day. She'd seen every kind of broken and destroyed body in the past several years. But now she was afraid for Graham. She took in a sharp breath.

He reached up a hand to touch her face, the marked side. His thumb touched her temple and cheek. He traced the edge of her mouth down to her chin. She closed her eyes in a slow blink, and she viewed him with a little more focus when she reopened her eyes.

He pulled her into his arms, and she buried her head against his chest.

"It's going to be all right," he whispered.

She shook her head, not in an attempt to say no, but to clear her thoughts. Ava loved the feeling of his breath on her hair.

"There *was* a man, but he wasn't really following me. My mind played tricks on me. I came back here to be safe. I didn't want to be alone." She took in a shaky breath. "I haven't been afraid of being alone until now. Now that you are here, I'm suddenly afraid. And then to find you out in the street. They were going to hurt you badly. I can't live like this anymore, Graham. I don't like the night anymore. I can't find order. I can't sleep. I can't dream. And if I do . . ."

A wave of feeling darted through her at her sad admission. He uttered her name, and she loved the sound of it coming from his mouth. It took all the strength she had not to say his name in return and replace those sounds with her lips touching his.

"Breathe," he ordered.

You must trust him.

He held her to him. She stood limply, neither pulling away nor deepening the embrace. He touched her shoulder, ran his hand along the back keeping her close to him. He ran has hands over her hair and traced each twist of hair that shrouded her face. "Are you feeling better?" he asked.

"No."

Then he would go on holding her.

Eventually she relaxed into his embrace; her arms tentatively slipped around his neck. She took in a deep breath and released a long pent-up sigh. Her first good breath and his last, because she leaned more comfortable against him, unaware that something in the embrace was changing.

He whispered to her, tender comforting words. Minutes passed, and Graham didn't break the spell between them. He brushed a kiss on her forehead. He held her for many moments, murmuring words she couldn't decipher. She was sinking further into his arms and wanted nothing more than his embrace. She could heal him. She could take away his cold. As though his body could read her mind, she felt him tense. Her hands had been quiet on his back, but she tentatively ran them up to his neck then down again to wrap around his waist.

He brought his mouth to hers, but instead of kissing her, he let his lips hover a breath away. She braced under the promise but refusal of his kiss. A wall rose up between them without a sound, anchored in the questions still to be answered.

Did my brother do this to you?

I'm afraid he might have.

She wrapped his chest in bandage. He seemed surprised by her strength as she pulled the edges tight. She could fix what was broken. She put him on the old beat-up sofa in the corner of the office and told him to close his eyes for a few minutes. She hoped he didn't have a concussion. When his eyes drifted closed, she touched her lips to his, and he opened his eyes again. They blinked once and closed again.

Please God, don't let me fall in love with him.

SINCE ALL THE men were bunked down for the night, Ava walked up to the television in the cafeteria. She'd been avoiding the news. They kept the volume turned down so the noise wouldn't bother the residents, and the captions scrolled up the screen. Wasn't the news the same as preaching? They were saying words and didn't care if the words were just to be said or if the words were to be heard. Soon enough, Joel's face flashed on the screen.

He had sandy brown hair with blond overtones. His eyes were pale hazel. Every other woman in the world would call him gorgeous. The only thing unusual about him was his olive skin tone. She imagined that as a child he was a towheaded boy marooned on a distant island. Sun-bleached hair, eyes like the setting sun, skin tanned by heat and warmth. That was a fairy tale she'd tell herself when she thought about forgiving him, but he'd grown up in Atlanta on the southside of the city. Angry father, rough neighborhood, mother who made do with what she didn't have. He'd turned to sports to avoid trouble and had done well enough to go to college on a football scholarship. He'd come back home a hero and first round draft pick. But the night Ava met him he got drunk for the first time in his life.

She'd been sober and sad. Something about her face made him angry. Something about her face had made him turn into an animal. Joel Sapphire was in hiding or maybe in some bar getting drunk, looking at the face of his next victim.

Lance walked over and stared at the television screen with her.

"Should we turn this off?" he asked.

She had never asked this question before, but she had to know. "What did I look like when you found me, Lance?"

"Ava . . ."

"I need to know. Please. Not the police version. What you really thought."

He moved to the television and turned it off.

"I thought you were dying. I thought I saw an angel or a light over you. But I was high and delirious." He started straightening the chairs stacked on the cafeteria tables even though they were already perfectly aligned. "No one should die alone. That's why I called out for help and held your hand and stayed by your side. I thought you were about to pass. It just as easily could have been me lying in an alley almost dead. I'd done nothing in my life to prevent it from happening. I thought if I were on the ground, I would want one more chance, I would want someone to get help and save me. Then when the police came and you were alive, I knew it wasn't a coincidence. That angel was for me and you. I prayed that you would make it like I never prayed for anything in my life. I knew if you survived, I would, too."

"Do you believe Joel Sapphire attacked me?" she asked.

"Yes." He paused. "Don't you?"

"I don't know."

"Well, you are good to try and forgive him. If you knew all the things I've done in my life, I'd hope you'd forgive me. His brother is a good man. I never seen a white man seem to care that much about a place like this. It is work, not words, that matter. He's focused on this shelter like he owes the place something.

Lance walked away, and Ava felt the room dim. The light he spoke about over her body was him. What if the most courageous thing you do is hold a dying person's hand? That would be enough. Ava had held her father's hand, and she didn't have enough light to keep him alive. But she never let him go.

The empty cafeteria room was illuminated by a red neon exit sign. According to her mother, this shelter was where Ava would die. The chairs stacked upside down on the tables made dark silhouettes against the walls that looked like crucifixes. In order to die, you had to be alive.

While Graham slept, she would finish what he started. They were different. He only wanted to prove that his brother was innocent. Ava wanted the truth. She thought she wanted the truth, but she remembered how right it felt to stand in Graham's arms. Did she want the truth, or did she want Graham? Could she love him if his brother was guilty?

Chapter 22

ELLIOT OPENED THE door to the house and frowned at Ava. The scent of grilled hot dogs and chili rushed out of the house.

"May I speak to Mr. Sapphire's mother?"

Elliot didn't welcome her in but allowed her access and led her to the television room. Wendy Sapphire turned to watch them walk in. She nodded and smiled with a sigh. "Ava, I've been waiting to meet you. Please forgive me if I don't get up."

Wendy sat on the sofa with her feet propped up on the table in front of her. She was thin in a way that was new to her. She used to be a woman with curves and a glow to her skin.

Ava nodded at her without saying a word.

"Good," Wendy continued. "We don't allow much talking during football games, and I'm afraid it's a big game tonight. I'm Wendy Sapphire. We love football around here. Quinn and Elliot are busy making lunch, and I'd be happy if you stayed. Do you like football?"

"I never watch it much, I'm afraid," Ava said. She felt like a visitor from another planet.

Wendy wrapped a fuchsia blanket around her. She wore a blue knit cap on her head. "What kind of woman are you? You grew up around here, right? Football is life. Man or woman. If you sit next to me, I can teach you the basics."

"I'm not staying that long," Ava said. Her hand drifted to a stack of books on the table next to Wendy.

"Why are you here?"

"I don't know."

"Then tell me about Graham. I haven't seen him since yesterday," Wendy said. "You must love him."

"I—we just met."

Not true. He's written to me for seven years.

Wendy watched Ava's expression turn uncomfortable. "No, I don't mean that." The woman's musical laughter filled the air, but she turned back to Ava and allowed her smile to fade. "Oh, dear. I didn't expect all of that. Is that why you are here? Because of Graham?"

Ava picked up a book with a Viking on the cover. It would be so much easier to fall in love with him.

"I'm here because of you."

She heard Graham's soft voice. *I'm here because of my brother, and I'm here because of you.*

"I didn't realize you were in treatment. Graham didn't mention it, and he should have since my brother-in-law is an oncologist, and I thought you could talk to him if you need a second opinion. His name is Dr. Wesley. He's at the university hospital in the cancer center. Really one of the best doctors if you want to base anything on my personal bias."

"He's a good brother-in-law?"

"Yes. He takes good care of my sister. Coaches my niece's soccer team. Helps my mother find men for me to date."

"Sounds like my kind of man. Jack of all trades. Got to paint, cook, clean, and save the world to survive."

Ava put down the book and turned to Wendy Sapphire. "What about us?"

"We have to do all the stuff they do and then some. Love football even when we're losing, read romance novels but never worry over love, forgive, find beauty, laugh, if we're lucky, have babies. If we are really lucky, we don't have babies." She laughed again. "I don't mean that to be mean, but kids aren't for everyone. We don't all follow the same path to happiness, and we have to hope our friends will remind us to laugh when we can't." She sighed and pulled off her hat. "I hate this thing."

With her head bare of hat or hair, her face became luminous hazel eyes and a wide smile. "I need a hat that matches team colors, but I wear this blue one because Graham bought it for me. He doesn't like my head to be cold."

"You said you haven't seen him today?" Ava asked. Lance

had made sure he didn't have a concussion last night. "And . . . you haven't heard from Joel."

"Is that the real reason why you came to see me?"

Yes, until just now. Ava said. "I came to borrow some courage. I need to do something very brave. My mother is the bravest woman I know, but sometimes her strength makes me feel weak. And Graham. He talks about you all the time. He never once mentioned you were sick, but I thought I should meet you. I thought I might borrow some bravery from you. And some happiness."

Wendy laughed. "I'm not brave. I used to be dead in my other life. Dying now doesn't make me a bit afraid. And happiness I steal from everywhere. When you said those things about your brother-in-law and you picked up that book. When you called your mother brave. It is hard to realize when you are being happy, and I steal it when I see it in other people. You should do the same."

Ava nodded.

"That's not enough. You have to stay and watch football with me. Just for a little while. You leaving is fear. You leaving isn't looking for happiness. I know you are scared of us. You are more scared of being inside this warm, wild house than you are of anything out in the world."

Ava picked up the hat and ran her hand over the intricate crocheted pattern.

"Can you start by telling me the team colors? Then after that, you'll have to speak slowly and tell me everything twice."

Wendy grabbed her hand and gave it a squeeze. "Blue is my very favorite color, but on game days, it's best we wear red. For luck."

You are lucky.

It was hard to accept anything as luck when no matter what happened, someone was out there who hurt you, slashed your face, made you afraid of daylight and happiness. What if she could never find luck or happiness anywhere? What if she was only sad destinies for the rest of her life?

And next to her was Wendy. Dying maybe, but

sunshine-happy like Nadine. Everyone had an equal. If everyone could be brought low, then everyone could rise up.

She could buy a red dress. She could watch a little football with Graham's mother. With Joel's mother.

It'd had been a long time since Ava made a new friend.

Chapter 23

THE WALKWAY IN front of Martin Brown's house had seventeen cracks between the street and the doorstep. Ava felt the weight of the cement under her feet and had a hard time catching her breath. In, guilty. Out, innocent. Ava shook her head at her shoes, the hair fell forward, and she swept it to the left. When she looked up, half of her face was revealed. She had fifty-eight minutes to speak to Martin Brown and get back outside to her car. She had to be at the shelter by 4:01 p.m. She could be earlier but not later. It was her habit to break any day other than today.

If Ava was late even by a minute, Brad Vargas would show up. Brad thought it a waste of time. Graham didn't know she was there. It wasn't a lie if she didn't say where she would be. He'd been banged up bad enough to still be sleeping it off in her office, Lance said. Good. This was her chance to speak to Martin alone.

She was in a blue turtleneck, skirt, and high-heeled boots. It was the first time she'd worn anything other than black in years. The vibrant color suited her skin, but she was cold to the touch. Hesitation made her stride stilted and slow. She was afraid.

She allowed a small smile to touch her lips.

Someone could be watching. I'm ready to find out a different truth. Why can't I go back to my sweet midnights of sirens and broken bodies?

She rang the doorbell, and Martin Brown welcomed her into his house with a large smile. Ava immediately became calm. Her heart raced like the wings of butterfly. She could fly. She could escape her fear. Her hair covered her scars, and she shook Martin's hand with a smile.

They sat in the living room. A pop radio station played in the background, which seemed the unlikely choice for a man who looked like a bodybuilder. Blond hair, brown eyes, orange fake tan. The television showed an infomercial about a vegetable juicing machine. Ava could see the kitchen around the corner and saw carrots diced in perfect small circles on a plate with stump and tip still there. A serrated knife made for slicing bread lay across the plate.

"Thank you for seeing me." She paused for a moment and channeled her mother's calm, deliberate way of speaking. *If you want the truth, don't ask for it. Make the other person trust you enough to reveal it.*

"Mr. Brown, I wanted to see you before the media descended. Eventually Joel Sapphire will come out of hiding, and people will want to talk to you. To all of us. I needed to thank you for what you did those years ago. I'm sorry it's taken me so long to meet you. You helped the police and the trial. My family and I owe you a debt of gratitude."

Slow down.

She wore her pearl necklace but did not touch a bead.

Please, God. I don't know what I'm praying for.

"Your father was very generous, Ms. Camden."

"You own a liquor store now, I understand?"

"Yes. My brother-in-law runs it for me. I've got a cabin up in Helen. I don't mean to sound like I'm leading the soft life because of your . . . you know. I didn't ask for any payment. Your father insisted."

"I understand. You don't have to explain. You saved my life. You deserve everything a man dreams of. Security, freedom." She nodded at a photograph of a cabin on a lake. "You have a boat, too?"

"No boat. I can't swim. As for freedom, I don't know who has freedom, but I'm lucky." He laughed and pointed a finger at his head and pulled the imaginary trigger. "I have everything I need right here in this house. And about me saving you . . . I did what anyone would do. Can I get you some water?"

Ava tried to breathe evenly. The house had an overwhelming scent of bleach. It was like sitting in a dried out swimming pool.

"No, thanks. Did Joel Sapphire's brother come and talk to you? I heard a rumor from some of my friends on the police force."

"Yeah, that guy came by. Asked me if there was anything I might have forgotten. I told him no. He wasn't any bother, but I did let the police know. He shouldn't stir up trouble."

"People are going to ask you again if you have any doubts about Joel Sapphire being the attacker. I hope you understand how important your words are. There are those who say he didn't do it, but you're the only person who could say for certain."

Martin shook his head. "He was there. I saw him in the alley with you. It was a terrible night."

"Well, it's possible that those people might ask you to recant your story. I want to make sure you don't. I don't want you to say somebody else could have done this to me."

Ava stared directly at Martin, her eyes on him without wavering.

He laughed. "Of course, I wouldn't say somebody else did it."

She breathed. In, guilty. And held her breath. Out, innocent. "Do you mind telling me what happened that night? I've never heard it directly from you. Even when you testified in court . . . it was hard for me to listen. I tuned out."

"Sure." He leaned forward, his hands expressive, his face solemn. "So I was coming out of the rear storage area when . . ."

A shadow moved in the hallway as Martin started talking. Ava didn't turn her head, but in the periphery of her vision she saw a woman open a door and look out. Ava tried to keep her gaze on Martin. A child darted into the hallway, picked up a ball, and darted back into the room. The door closed again quickly. Ava started counting.

One kitchen table.

One chair.

Zero picture frames.

Zero vases.

Zero paper weights.

Zero trophies.

All the surfaces were bare. No glasses or plates out in the kitchen. Only the carrots and the wrong knife. Same snack time as in her sister's house. Carrots diced for a child but no toys. No books. Sofa and chair and table all bare. But there were cameras. Five cameras there. Four there. And that picture of the cabin on the lake.

"You're a photographer?" Ava asked.

"It's my hobby," he said.

One set of keys. Too many keys that jangled like bells. Too many doors that needed locking.

Martin leaned in. ". . . I walked past the alley and saw a guy struggling over something. I didn't know who you were. I mean I didn't know it was you. I shouted to find out what was going on, and he ran. He ran with the knife and blood. He was fast, you know, and I'm not a runner. I ran after him as long as I could. He crossed into the mall parking lot, and that's where the police found him. I didn't want him to get away."

I didn't want him to get away.

"He didn't struggle. Did he?"

"No, he didn't. He was sooo drunk."

Very slowly, very casually, she moved the hair away from her face. The line of Martin's gaze was on her scars, and he sat back and exhaled. Everyone else inhaled when they saw her face, but he seemed curious.

"Thank you," she said.

Eight sets of dumbbells on the floor.

Four locks on the outside of the bedroom door.

Nothing could be broken.

Everything smelled like bleach.

The door opened and closed down the hallway again. The woman made sure Ava could see her face then shut the door again.

The world stopped.

"I don't want to disturb your family, Martin. I should get going."

He stood up. "That's my wife and son. He's got a lot of

homework. I'll be right back."

Ava stood. Another door opened and closed before Martin returned. The music was up louder, because that's how people argued. Martin was wearing an apologetic smile. She was so calm she felt as if she'd left her body. "Thank you again, Martin. My mother might contact you. She'll eventually find out that Joel Sapphire's brother was here, and she'll appreciate you keeping your cool. She can be generous in her gratitude. If you wouldn't mind indulging her, it would make us all very happy."

"Of course, of course. Glad to see you are doing better. Nice to see you, Ava."

Ava shook his hand, and Martin gave a challenging grip that caused her a moment of pain.

With his grim look of approval, Martin Brown tried to shatter her world. He could not, but the shadowed eyes at the end of the hallway could. Ava no longer needed saving. Someone else did.

The woman in Martin Brown's house had been the bartender that night.

The bartender was the same woman who ran out of her father's office on the night he died. She had tried to get help from Cecil Camden, tried to tell him the truth, but he turned her away. Why? Memories of her father came flooding back.

She's nobody. She's a liar.

Why didn't he listen to her?

Because Joel Sapphire had already been convicted. Because to re-open the case then would expose all that Cecil Camden had done—ethically and otherwise—to make sure someone was punished for the attack on his daughter. It never mattered that Joel was white. It mattered that Joel was the first suspect, and in Cecil's experience, the first suspect usually ended up being the best suspect. Ava's father would not admit he'd sent an innocent man to prison. Rather than ruin his own career, he'd let the monster who destroyed her face remain free.

He'd rather die.

Ava walked slowly down the steps. The bartender . . . Paige . . . could tell fortunes from the lines she remembered in books. Ava wished she could see the future or the past. The crevices in the cement looked like the lines in a human palm. Suddenly there were cracks and broken places everywhere.

Chapter 24

SHE OPENED THE curtains even though no sunlight came in. A storm darkened the afternoon sky. Ava held in her tears and spoke quietly to Graham on the phone. She walked though her house, feeling the emptiness of it for the first time.

"Can you come see me? I want you to stay with me tonight. I don't care what you think that means. I can't go to the shelter. I can't be alone. I need you, Graham."

She took a breath and tried not to cry.

For a long moment, he was silent on the other end of the phone.

"Of course. I'll be there in a little while," he said and hung up without saying goodbye.

Ava walked out onto the back deck. The autumn air that had been cold was suddenly hot. A storm loomed, and it brought the final warm days before winter. As children, she and Nadine had called it pumpkin summer, because they didn't know what those warm days were called. The leaves had turned from green to yellow and orange, and then just before winter started, summer returned for a few days.

In the middle of the yard was the oak tree that had been hit by lighting. It would need to come down. Like the deleted pictures. And the shelter. Some things would need to end. Other things would have to go on.

Ava lay back on a lounge chair and closed her eyes. She heard thunder in the distance and the rain began. When she felt the first drop of water on her face, she allowed herself to cry.

Joel went to jail for nothing.

I've been hating the wrong man all these years.

It felt good to cry, and she lost track of how long she was out in the storm.

"What are you doing out here?" Graham asked in hushed tones. "I tried knocking and then walked around the back."

The rain increased in intensity, and she hadn't heard him approach. Each drop made a different sound.

"I love the rain," she said, but when he tried to pull her to standing, she resisted. "I need to stay. I think I can count every drop." Ava turned her face back up toward the sky. Rain fell onto her upturned face. She smiled at the clouds like she was basking in the sun.

"Ava?" he asked. The rain dampened her hair. It fell down the back of the chair toward the ground in long dark waves. Her entire face was exposed to the rain and to Graham's gaze. "What are you doing out here?" He asked again, but this time didn't try to pull her inside.

"When I was a kid, my mother never let us play in the rain. She didn't want us to catch a cold or ruin our clothes or mess up the floors in the house. She had a million reasons why puddles were meant to be avoided. Why was the rain forbidden to us as children?" She turned to look at him. Her face was covered in wet sadness, and he swallowed.

"The rain is nice," he said quietly.

"It feels like tears," she said, turning her face back to the sky. Thunder rolled in the distance, but there was no lightning. "The rain feels like tears on my face." She smiled a true smile. "And I like it."

In that moment, she could be safe. In an afternoon rain shower. Safe in the shadows. Safe being alone. Safe with him. Safe with her tears.

"Why are you crying?" he asked.

"I'm confused. Everything is confusing me. When I forget to be angry it's like I've lost my anchor. I can't find solid footing without it. I'm crying because I'm glad you are here. And it's the last warm night before winter comes. That always makes me sad."

She covered her face, and deep wrenching sobs escaped from her. She wanted to scream at the sky. She had faced her attacker alone, and Graham could not know yet what she'd done or what she'd discovered. If he knew, he would kill Martin Brown and be lost to her. She stood up and reached for his hand. She led him into the house, and the tears continued to slip from her eyes.

She'd wanted him to wrap his arms around her since the night he'd walked into the shelter looking lost. Nobody as beautiful as he could ever love her.

Graham pushed the hair away from her face as he embraced her. His hands traced the line of her ear and the length of her shoulder. He should leave her, but Ava found herself looking up and trembling and holding onto his shirtfront, because if she wrapped her arms around him, if she pressed her body against him, she would be truly lost in his scent and heat.

She should have told him something then. She should have said everything would be all right. That she loved him, but she didn't know what would happen in a day or a week. She didn't know if she could recognize love coming from her.

He rubbed his hands down her back. His heart beat directly beneath her ear. His breath washed over the top of her head. He slid his hands into her hair and tilted his face to hers. She opened her eyes, and his were waiting for her. Like he wouldn't kiss her until she knew it was him and why he was kissing her and why she was more scared in that moment than any other.

Graham never swore, but he cursed with his mouth a breath away from hers.

His eyes stayed open and until he touched his lips to hers. She slid her arms around his neck, and he relaxed. It was the quietest kiss. He tasted her mouth without deepening the kiss. She didn't know that two lips touching could be so shattering. She realized that she could heal him with her embrace and with her kiss.

He kissed her slowly, devouring little sections of her mouth with his tender caress. Something in her died. It was the anger. When he would eventually leave her life, Ava didn't want to be angry at him. She wanted to look back on the moments of her life, moments of terror and passion, and not be afraid. And not have regrets.

She led him to her room, and he stopped when he saw the mirrors that covered walls. Each reflection was a different part of them. With and without scars. With and without tears. What had seemed insane became beautiful as she pulled off her wet clothing. She stood before him in only her underwear and pushed him on the bed. She leaned over him. She was afraid he was going to stop and pull away from her, but he slid a hand behind her neck and brought her mouth to his. He shifted beneath her and changed how their bodies touched. Her mouth fell open with a small escape of air, and he stole her breath with his lips and tongue.

"Tell me what happened," he said. "Something happened today that made you change. I want to know what."

"I think your brother is innocent," she said.

"Why? What did you learn?" he asked.

"Nothing. I learned nothing. You've convinced me. I don't think he did it."

Graham sat up and looked around the room. She straddled his waist. Even though he stopped kissing her, his hands continued to stroke her back and hair.

"Is he conveniently innocent so you can have sex with me?" he asked.

"No, of course not."

Ava felt like she'd been slapped. She slid off his lap. She'd been ashamed of her face for a long time but stood before him proud of her body. "Even with my scars, I can get a man. Men are simple creatures. Offer them sex, and they'll forget that you are dumb or fat or ugly or poor. They'll forget you have scars. They'll ignore the fact that you are half insane. I don't need you for sex." She felt tears in her eyes even without the rain. "I want you. Don't get me wrong. I want only you. I want you to kiss me and hold me and tell me I'm not crazy anymore. Do you know how hard it is for me to accept that Joel is innocent? Have you ever considered for a moment that he is guilty, the way I've had to imagine he is innocent? What would you do if everything you believed turned out to be a lie?"

"If he attacked you, I would accept it."

"You would accept it and leave me."

Graham went to the window. Because of the storm, it was another kind of mirror.

"Yes, I would leave you alone if he were guilty."

"Why do you feel guilt for something you didn't do? It isn't about your brother at all. I could spit in your face, and you'd say 'Thank you.' I could cut you or hit you, and you would take my rage. Because of your father? Why?"

Graham turned. His eyes went cold. Ava could feel the restrained anger coming off of him. "Don't ever suggest that I am serving my own purposes. I have given up everything I've ever wanted in life to make sure Joel could be happy. My mother worked hard, two and three jobs at a time, to support us. We have slept in the park and under overpasses. I was the one who raised my brother. I protected him. Any faults he has are mine. Not our father's. We don't carry any of his evil in us. I want to believe my brother. I don't want to be wrong about this," he whispered.

"You won't believe that I want to be with you because you are kind," she said hoarsely, "because you have helped me when everyone else pitied me. What if I cared for you regardless of your brother?" She walked up to a mirror but didn't see her face. She only saw his back silhouetted in the storm.

"What should I believe?" he asked. "I can't believe he hurt you."

"You don't have to believe he hurt me." She turned. Her own calm façade fading, and her eyes now an angry reflection of his own. "Accepting that he is innocent is difficult for me. I've had to change."

"You're right," he said hoarsely. "I have had to change, too. I have considered that he is guilty. That's why I tried to stay away from you. If he is guilty of ever laying a hand on you, if he is guilty of ever hurting you, I would kill him myself."

"Then why doubt me if I say that he didn't do it. Because you have to keep me away. That's what changed, Graham. I believe and you don't. If I kissed you today and you found out he did it, you'd leave me."

"I would."

"I wouldn't," she said. She turned and found his eyes. "I wanted to kiss you last night. I never thought that any man would want me the way you do. That's why I've been crying. I care about you no matter where you came from or what your brother did." She held out her hand. "Please don't go away."

He walked toward her and stroked the hair that surrounded her face. "I love you, Ava. I don't think I can ever leave you, but it isn't for me to decide. It is your choice. You have to decide. I want a wife and a lover and a partner who can't see my scars. I don't care if you work in a homeless shelter or as a photographer or at a law firm. I care that you are brave for me and everyone who walks into The Light House."

She reached into her nightstand and pulled out a stack of letters. Each envelope carefully open and the letter preserved with care. Interspersed with his letters were corresponding ones from her.

"I wrote you back. Angry, sad, afraid. I've been talking to you for years. I trust you. I want you to trust me when I say I'll try to help your brother."

She dropped the letters on the nightstand. She thought he'd reach for them, but he reached for her instead. She ran her hands over his wide shoulders and the length of his arms. She felt the mark of the Greek letter on his bicep. She reached up and pulled him down for another kiss. Graham teased her with his tongue. He picked her up and laid her on the bed and traced his fingers over her body. He bent to kiss her again, touching her breasts, stroking her soft flesh delicately. Ava let out a small gasp at the intimacy of his touch and gaze. She felt her body turn to liquid and then fire and then explode and float away.

Ava wanted to learn his body, too. She paused at the brand on his arm. "How could you let someone burn you after what your father did to you?"

"I didn't want him to have the last word. I didn't want to live my life afraid of fire. I wanted my frat brothers to know I was as strong as they were. They didn't all do it. If I ever have a son, I don't think I'd let him do it, but each person has their own reason. Why do people tattoo their bodies or pierce their ears?"

"We are never satisfied with our own beauty," she said.

He put his hands behind his head, and Ava traced the muscles of his chest as she lay on top of him. Ava rested her head on his chests. He started to smile. "I'm beautiful because I'm wearing you."

Graham closed his eyes and held her to him for a few moments before rolling them both onto their sides.

"Sleep?" she asked.

"Kiss then sleep," he compromised. Then he kissed her like sleep was the last thing on his mind.

Chapter 25

THE EARLY MORNING sunlight reflected off the mirrors on the bedroom walls and created a kaleidoscope of color and shadow on Graham's face. He opened his eyes to the cold pillow beside him and the deathly quiet of the house. Ava was gone. Down the hallway he could see light streaming out of the other empty rooms. The house that used to be closed curtains and gloom transformed into light and wide open windows. Outside, orange and red foliage fell like snowflakes, but the steady flurry seemed unnatural. He was trapped in a strange world of glass and silence.

Ava should not be gone. She should be at his side the way she had been during the night. Her stillness and heat a comfort to him. He loved the feel of her breath against his neck and later, her bodying curving into his. Graham listened for her in the bathroom but heard nothing. The floors had a habit of echoing every step, and the walls echoed each breath breathed. Instead the air was silent. She wasn't only gone from the room, she was gone from the house.

He sat up. Ava had left a red gift bag on the nightstand. Graham pulled out a bundle of tissue paper and unwrapped a photo of Ava in a crimson frame. Her face frozen, her eyes exhausted. The three long scars down her face looked like rain. It was almost impossible for him to see the scars on her in life, but she was finally captured on film. All Graham could see was the brutality of the attack.

A photo could not capture the willow-like movements of her hair, her soft mouth, and forgiving eyes. Those eyes shed so many tears last night. Her mind battling between sadness and love. He remembered her deep aching sobs and touched her face in the picture. Graham would find whoever did this to her. He would make that person pay for what they did. Why had she been crying? Where had she gone?

He opened and clenched his fists.

I love the feeling of rain on my face. He isn't guilty.

He felt a slow building terror. She'd found her real attacker. Graham pulled a note out of the bag. The message wasn't for him.

> *Dear Lexi and Lydia,*
>
> *Please remember me and how much I always loved you.*
>
> *Aunt Ava.*

Loved.

Not love.

Where had she gone?

Graham pulled on his shoes. He'd spent his life allowing the memory of his father to hurt him, but now Ava could hurt him, too. Her absence. Her fear. Her being in danger. Graham would be destroyed if she was lost to him.

He opened and closed his fists again. She'd once thought he was looking for dirt on his hands, but he was looking for blood.

His phone was flashing on the nightstand. Ava must have turned off the ringer and put the gift bag on top of it.

The message came in an hour before.

Martin Brown did this to me. I have to get to him before you, Joel, or the police. I'm sorry, Graham. Go to his house.

AVA STOPPED IN the alley behind the old restaurant before doing anything else. An employee from the new place sat on a crate next to a propped open door. The woman was using her break to read something on her phone.

Maybe she read a book.

Have all things sad destinies?

Maybe she exchanged messages with her spouse.

I want a wife and a lover and a partner.

Ava thought the alley would be empty. Wherever she sought solitude, she was never alone. Suddenly that wasn't a bad thing. There was safety in numbers greater than one and sanity in knowing that everyone healed. If everyone has scars, there are two choices. Bleed to death slowly or stitch yourself together.

"There used to be a restaurant here," Ava said.

"I remember that place," the woman said. "That was a long time ago."

"What is this place now?" Ava asked.

She tried to peer into the doorway and saw clothes in the window at the store front.

"Consignment shop. Designer stuff. We don't sell any junk," the woman said. She glanced from her phone to Ava. The woman stood up when their eyes met. "You come here a lot?"

"You recognize me?"

"The news has been running pictures of you since . . . the past few days."

"I've never been back here. Not since that night." She paused and looked at the dumpster and empty crates. The ground was clean, and everything could be counted. "I remember it differently."

The sound of bells were his keys. He had the keys to the restaurant and all those locks.

Ava looked at the surrounding walls. Lance had found her because there was a light over her body. An angel. She looked up, turned in a slow circle, and stopped at the point where she knew her body had been. Ear pressed toward hell. Eyes looked toward heaven. There was a security camera.

"At least you have better security now," Ava said.

"That old thing? No one has ever taken it down. Ours is over the door," the woman said. Ava looked up and saw a mirror the size of a postcard at the keystone of the doorway. "That's it."

I thought you were dying. I thought I saw an angel or a light over you.

It had been recording. She pulled out her phone. It was a long shot. A very long shot, but she knew what she had to do.

"Martin, this is Ava Camden. I'm sorry to bother you again." Her stomach clenched with a pain. *He did this to me, but it wasn't to hurt me. It was to hurt someone else.* "Is it okay if I come over to your house?"

Ava counted the cracks in the sidewalk. When she stopped finding broken lines, she would be face to face with Martin again.

GRAHAM JUMPED into his truck and sped toward Ava. There was no good reason why Martin would have attacked her. He was the manager of a restaurant, and she was a stranger—just another customer. By everyone's account they had no connection, but Graham always doubted everyone's version of the truth. Especially Martin's, who never saw the attack, and the dull acceptance of everyone else that Joel did it just because he was there. Cecil Camden had rewarded any witness. His appreciation meant that every hand he shook received a payment of gratitude in cash.

Graham punched a number into the phone as he drove.

"Officer Vargas, did Ava Camden contact you this morning?" he asked.

"I am sleeping. And off-duty. Who is this?"

"Graham Sapphire. Don't hang up. I think she's in danger. She's gone to see Martin Brown. Again. Did she call you?"

"Hang on," Brad ordered. There was shuffling in the background. A dog barked. "Obi-wan, quiet down girl. Shit. She called. Hang on. Hang on."

"I'm on my way to Martin's house. I can't let her be alone with him. The man tried to kill her. Here is what everyone has avoided saying for all these years. He tried to kill her. She wasn't just attacked. She was almost murdered."

"I know what happened to her, Graham. I can't listen to her message on the other phone with you shouting in my ear. Do not go to that house," Brad said.

Graham stepped on the accelerator, but he kept quiet. Until Vargas started swearing again.

"Shit. Shit. Meet me by the Amtrak station. The corner of Deering and Peachtree. His house is only a few blocks behind there," Brad said.

"What'd she say?" Graham asked.

"She says there's a woman and a boy locked in the house. Locked in like they haven't seen the light of day in years. Ava says if we go to the back of the house we'll hear the music turned up loud all the time, but there is a small window she can fit through in the back of the house. She's going in."

Graham swerved into the left lane to avoid colliding with a bus. "She's going to kill him, Brad. Should you call backup or something?"

"Where we're going isn't my precinct. I'm sleeping. I'm off-duty. I may or may not be grabbing the keys to my motorcycle. Twenty minutes."

"I can't wait twenty minutes."

"I'll be there in ten."

Graham circled past the house and did not see Ava's car anywhere on the street. He looped around the block and to the train station and still nothing. He would give Vargas nine minutes then he was going in.

Brad got there in eight, and Graham knew better than to ask the man what laws of nature he broke to get there that fast. Heat emanated from the tire tread of the motorcycle.

Graham and Brad knocked on the front door but didn't wait for an answer. They ran around to the back of the house. The yard was fenced and locked, but whoever had been there before them had already broken the lock on the gate. The yard was empty, no lawn furniture. No dog to warrant the locked gate and sign that said Beware Of Dog. The small window Ava mentioned was not disturbed. It was covered with a piece of plywood they tore off to reveal a window too small for either of the men to consider using. It was covered with butcher paper, so even though they could hear music playing in the house, they couldn't see in.

There was a sound like the mewing of a cat. Then another louder sound like a cry for help.

The train line intersected the end of the street. The squealing of wheels in the distance meant a freight train approached. A commuter train also ran along the same corridor, creating noise in the neighborhood.

You needed noise outside and in to drown out screams.

Graham looked down at his boots covered in red clay. It wasn't the first time he smashed in a window. He kicked his foot through the glass. The music spilled into the yard with an angry fervor.

"Is anybody in there?" he shouted and crouched down. With the morning light behind him and the darkness within, he couldn't see anything. "Ava?"

Graham looked back at Brad who was shaking his head.

When he turned back to the broken window, he was surprised to see the face of a small boy, eye-level with him, and a woman's voice coming from the shadows. "Take him, please."

The boy reached toward Graham, and Brad swore.

"Give him to me," Graham ordered. "I've got him." The child weighed nothing, but he was long, like his age and weight were not aligned. "Is Martin in the house with you?" Graham whispered into the darkness.

"I don't know. We can't hear him coming and going, but he's usually at the gym in the morning. He'll be back soon. Never the same time. You've got to get me out."

"Give me your hand. Did someone else come by today? This morning. A lady?"

"Not since yesterday. She was here, and he forgot to lock us in. But I don't think she came back. Did she tell you to come? I can't reach. I'm not tall enough. I can't get out."

"Stand on something."

"We don't have anything."

Graham could see a few sheets on the floor. No bed. No chairs. No tables. It smelled like a locker room. No air.

He turned to Brad who held the child to his side while he spoke quietly into the phone.

"We've got to come get you through the front door."

"No, he'll be back. He'll kill us. He won't let us go. Don't leave me. Don't go away."

Graham paused to think.

"Then give me a sheet. That's right, give me the ends, and you step your foot into the loop. I'll pull you high enough that you can grab hold of me. Okay, you're strong. You can do it."

The woman put her arms around his neck. He pulled her up, and she was weightless like the boy. Graham felt like he could carry anything in the world. She was trembling like it was so very cold, but inside the house was unnaturally warm. Graham grabbed her, and she slipped through the window like a newborn colt. She'd soon be standing, but for a moment she clung to the ground. Grass against one cheek. Sun against the other.

"Brad, you get them away. I've got to go inside."

"I've called for backup now."

"I can't wait another ten minutes to find Ava."

"Give me three, Graham. We've need to do this right."

"There is no right. Nothing is ever right."

He took off his jacket. It was the first time he'd remembered to wear one in weeks. He covered the woman on the ground. "You've got to get up as fast as you can. You need to be gone before he gets back. No one is ever going to hurt you again."

She nodded and whispered, "The grass is so soft and so cold." But she jumped to her feet without effort and reached for her son. The boy still clung to Vargas. "Are we okay?" she asked.

The child nodded, and the woman started crying. Brad pulled the butcher paper in place and hurried them through the broken fence. He tried to put the wood in place so it didn't look as broken. They just needed enough time to get away. Brad walked them toward the back of a neighboring house while Graham ran to the front door and kicked it in. A security siren went off, and in the distance, police sirens approached.

He ran into every room. The kitchen and house were clean enough by being empty. Graham opened every door. Then moved to a locked door that led to the basement. He opened each latch and found the room where the woman and boy were held. The music continued to blare.

Graham wanted quiet. Ava wouldn't like all the noise. He shouted her name, but she didn't answer. Down the hall was another locked door. He unlatched each bolt, but when the final lock fell away, the door won't budge. It was also secured from the other side.

Graham released a bellow that shook the foundation of the house. Music still played, and the siren sounded. He beat on the door. In his mind it was Martin Brown. He shoved his shoulder against the hinges. He punched and kicked the barrier like it was his father, and today would be the day all his hurts would go away.

He needed the police to break down the door. He couldn't save her alone. Graham fell to the ground and shouted for help.

"I'm over here. She's in here."

He looked at the clock. A few hours ago he held her in his arms. Now it was 8:01 a.m. It was the normal hour that Ava went to sleep.

A couple of officers rushed down the hall to Graham. He sat slumped on the ground next to the door. When he looked up, he recognized one of the officers. He didn't feel any anger about the beating he took in front of the shelter. They were looking out for Ava. And now he needed them.

"Can you open the door?" Graham asked.

The officer nodded. He held a battering ram in one hand and reached down with the other to pull Graham to standing.

"We thought you were the threat, Ice."

"Break down the door," Graham said.

It took four swings to break down the door. On the other side was a bedroom with a bathroom attached. It would have seemed a normal room for a guy, except the ropes, handcuffs, and overwhelming scent of bleach. Whatever happened in that room involved blood and clean up. A side door lead to another exit. That must have been how Martin left. Graham could only hope that Ava had never been there.

AVA NORMALLY WENT to Piedmont Park in the shadowy hours before dawn, but the sun was up as she waited for Martin Brown. And she was alone. She'd never thought about the window of time between the night dwelling runners and the day time warriors. When she needed people to protect her, none were there. The grass in the meadow had yellowed. The evergreen trees hid among the changing leaves. Red, yellow, orange. Ava noted the stench of the ginko tree and the sweetness of pine like the difference between guilt and innocence.

She picked up a large rock and slipped it into her pocket. The flattened piece of granite was about the size of an aluminum can. It had not been weathered or reduced by time. The edges of the stone were still jagged and sharp.

She could only hope that Graham and Brad had done what she needed them to do. Paige being safe was all that mattered. The woman knew enough about that night to testify against Martin. Ava didn't care about Joel's conviction or her scars. Those things were wounds to be healed on another day, but Martin had to be stopped today. Forever.

She'd seen people die. She'd seen the terrible effects of accident and rage. Ava knew death better than anything. She was the one who could make him pay.

Martin was supposed to meet her on the dock of Lake Clara Meer. He approached with the sun illuminating his face, and he waved at her with a smile, and he descended the steps into the shadows.

"Hey," he shouted from the distance. "I got here as fast as I could."

She nodded. She had enough time to glance at her phone and see a message from Graham. Any words she wanted to say to Martin died in her throat.

She is safe.

"You said Joel found you," Martin continued. "He called you?"

Please, God. Help me find my voice.

She nodded again.

Why did you hurt me? Why did you leave me for dead? This isn't who I was supposed to become. I'm not a monster. I don't hate. I'm not afraid.

"Ava, did Joel call you?"

"Actually, his attorney called me. I'm going to meet Joel today. He says he has something he needs to tell me."

"You aren't going to see him alone after what he did to you?"

Ava felt a smile touch her lips. In the middle of the lake, a flock of geese swam in unison.

"I'm not stupid. I wouldn't go alone. Besides what could he tell me or the police that Paige hasn't already said?"

She began counting the geese.

One. Two. Three. Four. Five.

Martin stepped closer to her.

"I'm sorry. What did you say?" Martin asked. He wore pale blue jeans and a fitted white long-sleeved shirt that emphasized the girth of his arms.

The geese changed direction in the lake and started moving toward the dock where Ava and Martin stood.

Six. Seven. Eight. Nine. Ten.

She took one step closer to Martin. If he wanted to reach her, he'd have to come all the way out onto the dock.

"I said, I'm not stupid. I'm not going alone. Or did you want me to repeat something else?" Her voice rose in hope.

His scanned the amphitheater behind them and the empty walkways. "What did you say about Paige?" Martin asked. His lips barely moved.

"You can't hurt her or the boy any longer," Ava said. She tried to remember what she had ever been afraid of. Only the bright light of day and the absence of shadows. She slipped her hand into the pocket of her coat and wrapped her hand around the stone. She breathed in. "Why did you attack me? I didn't know you. I never did anything to deserve this."

"I don't know what you are talking about. I never touched you."

"Paige knew the truth. That's why you wouldn't let her out of your house. She tried to tell my dad, but he wouldn't listen.

You are sick and evil, and I hope you die in jail. I hope someone takes a knife to your skin and carves my name in your face."

"Shut up," he whispered. "You were just a spoiled little rich girl. I saw you that night. No one talked to you. You didn't have friends, but still Paige was jealous of you and fascinated by Joel. I could tell that by talking to you both that she was thinking about leaving me. I wanted to show her what I could do to her if she left me. I would never hurt her, but I had to remind her that I could. If I had to."

"You never hurt her?" Ava whispered. What terror had that woman experienced in the dark captivity of that house? "What you did to her was worse. She's the reason why you are going to jail and never getting out." Ava paused and said her next words carefully. "Someone else will love her and take care of her despite her wounds."

"She wouldn't say anything against me."

Ava reached into her pocket and pressed a button on her phone. "Why don't we ask the police what she said?"

Martin rushed Ava then, and she backed up a few steps before he reached her and tried to snatch the phone from her hands. It fell to the dock, but he didn't try to pick it up. Martin grabbed her by the neck, and she pulled her hand out of her pocket and swung the rock at his head. The sharp edge smashed into his temple, and she swung two more times quickly before he was able to subdue her attack.

"You are going to die," he said. Blood dripped from the side of his face and stunned him for a moment. Martin squeezed her throat, and Ava knew there was no way she was strong enough to escape him. She struggled but felt herself losing air. She didn't mind dying as long as she took Martin with her. She remembered the ghosts she carried with her recently.

The woman shot in her car at the hands of her boyfriend. The baby that died inside of her.

The man confused enough by life and despair to hope the water would take away his pain.

Los embrazados. The sirens in the distance. Martin would be captured, but could Ava survive another trial? It would kill her.

And Joel. And Paige. So she stopped fighting and let her body go limp.

Ava grabbed the front of Martin's shirt as she let her wet collapse to the ground. She leaned back over the edge of dock.

Only jump if you can fly. Or swim.

No boat. I can't swim.

The world went quiet as they entered the water. The lake had started out as a pond and was expanded by man in the 1800s. The water was always murky. They were sinking, and Ava knew the moment Martin started to panic, because he released her throat. The air she desperately needed was above, but she could not open her eyes under the water. All she could do was sense the erratic flailing of Martin's sinking body and swim away.

He grabbed a hold of her foot, but she kicked her feet and shed her coat. Once her ankle was free of his grip, she paused. He wasn't trying to kill her, but save himself. So was she. Ava kicked her feet until she reached the surface. The first sound she heard was sirens. Beautiful, beautiful sirens. But the dock seemed so far away, and the threat of Martin pulling her below, too real. She couldn't swim to safety, and she tread water as the police surrounded the lake.

The officers paused to survey the scene, but Graham pushed past them and dove into the lake. He slipped an arm around her waist and began to strong side crawl to the dock. Brad Vargas pulled her out of the water and into a quick embrace as he shouted for blankets.

Ava collapsed onto the dock. Brad reached down and pulled Graham from the water.

"She's safe," Brad said to Graham.

Graham shook his head and reached for Ava. Her weight clothes were cold against her skin, but she didn't tremble. She wrapped her arms around him. She heard the voices of the police and bystanders and dogs barking. The park was suddenly alive with people.

I was jogging across the bridge. I saw him attack her. He was choking her. I called the police right away. She was lucky they fell into the water.

He was crazy.

Once they went into the water, he never came up for air.

"Martin's still in the lake," Ava said to Brad.

He stood above them like an angel. "I'll call in the dive team," he said. But he didn't move to do anything until the blanket arrived and he draped warmth over Graham and Ava's shoulders.

AVA AND GRAHAM drove up to the abandoned high school and found the back parking lot closest to the football field. Grass grew in the crevices of pavement that used to be the track. The field was an overgrowth of weeds that sprung into wildflowers. In the distance, Joel ran and didn't let the wildness impede him. He jumped over patches of grass when he needed to. He was red-faced and sweaty and running angry. Ava recognized anger in people even at a distance.

Sometimes it was a woman at the coffee shop or a man passing her on the street. After seven years of living in anger, it had a taste. It had a smell.

They bent to get under the gate. The rusted lock made a sound unlike bells. It was a clanging gong behind her as she walked towards the field. Empty bleachers, empty sidelines. A month ago, she would have been afraid to see Joel, but now she was anxious. She had so many things to say and so few words.

As he rounded the far side of the track, he caught sight of them and slowed his running. He raised a hand to block the sun, but he knew who it was. His feet began to fail him. Each step he took was slower than the one before.

He had a face that used to be happy. There were lines from years of smiling still etched into his sad expression. But the lines were fading. He'd forgotten happiness the same way she'd embraced fear. Joel stopped a dozen yards away from her and glanced at his watch.

1:37 p.m.

"You're early," Joel said to his brother. "I thought we agreed three o'clock."

"I don't like being late," she answered.

She should have told him she couldn't wait. She spent the drive in the car practicing things she would say.

I'm sorry. We all have scars now. Yours are scars no one will ever see.

But the first words were from Graham.

"They caught him," he said. "Joel, look at me. The police found the guy who did this to Ava. And you."

She tucked her hair behind her ear. Joel immediately turned to look at the field and shook his head. He didn't want to see her scars or her eyes. He didn't want to see his brother. He lifted the hem of his shirt and wiped what she thought was sweat from his face. He open and closed his fist and kept shaking his head as though her scars weren't possible.

"Arresting someone isn't the same as convicting someone," Joel said. He held his body erect. He stood braced for the impact of unknown disappointments.

"He's dead," Ava offered. "He drowned this morning in Piedmont Park."

Weeds sprouted into flowers along the field. There was hell beneath her feet and heaven above. She wanted to press her face to the ground.

Joel turned his pale hazel eyes to Ava. "He'll never be dead." His voice was deep and distant. "How can he be dead? I need to kill him myself." Joel had more of a Southern accent than Graham. Football and prison had their share of good old boys. That lilt made her trust in him. "I shouldn't have said that."

Graham put a hand on Joel's shoulder. "I was in his house today. I know how you feel. If you saw the way he tortured his family, people he was supposed to love, you would want him to be in pain for a long time. But people like that love pain. He was sick and evil, and death was too kind for him."

Joel nodded and looked at Ava. Like Graham, Joel found her eyes first but then stared at her scars.

"Joel, I'm so sorry. I can't tell you sorry enough times for how much I hurt you over this," she said.

"Ava, you didn't do this to me. I've never hated you. Maybe I've hated, but not you. You were the only innocent person in this whole thing."

She thought of her father and shook her head. There would be another time for that discussion. That disappointment and betrayal. No one was free of guilt, even the dead.

She reached down and pulled up another patch of dandelions. Why were they weeds and not flowers? If she thought she could ever speak to ghosts, she'd have to count Joel among them. He wasn't of this earth. Something in him was dead past repair.

The wind in the air died down. The noise from birds and crickets went silent. There in the bright sun, Ava felt an unfamiliar burning in her eyes. For all these years it had been anger. Hatred but not sadness. That's why she hadn't cried even over her father's grave. The fall of tears on her cheeks now would feel different than rain. But she exhausted all of crying with Graham. The daylight stayed hot and painful on her face. She took a breath that went in shaky and realized that in all those awake nights, she'd forgotten the sun.

She stepped closer to see Joel's face. She looked up at him. He was all sadness. His eyes lacked color, and his features defied shape or form. If sadness had the form of a face or body, it was Joel Sapphire.

He looked up at the sky as though the burning light of the sun caused his tears.

"He said he was going to kill our mother if I contacted my family. I got letters while I was in prison. Photographs of my mother and Graham. The police checked Martin Brown more than once. He was squeaky clean. No arrests or trouble of any kind. All his employers said he came to work, did his job, and caused no trouble. How could he be the one? He didn't even have a parking ticket, but he tortured his family?" Joel turned to Graham.

Graham opened and closed his fists. "Apparently, the girlfriend was trying to break up with him, so he used the attack on Ava as a warning. A demonstration of just how far he'd go to punish a woman."

"Ava? How are you?" Joel asked. *I had an accident, but now I'm fine.*

"Terrible."

"Graham, how's mom?"

"Same." Graham could say worse. He would never say she was dying. "Who helped you disappear when you left prison?"

"The GBI. I've been working with them for some time. Martin didn't realize it, but his crazy letters were what got me out early. They didn't know who did it or who was contacting me. He was careful. They didn't know if the conviction could ever be overturned, but they had growing evidence I didn't attack Ava. The only way to keep you, Ava, and Mom safe was to keep quiet. Graham, after everything you've done for me, you were the first person I wanted to tell." He blinked rapidly. "You were the only one who believed in me."

Joel inhaled slowly. "At first I didn't have any memory of that night. We'd promised each other to never drink. Sapphire men do not have good genes when it comes to alcohol, but then I was upset about something else, and a shot of whiskey seemed like a good idea. Then ten shots seemed like a better idea. I *still* have no memory of that night."

"Now we know with certainty," Ava said.

"Why are you looking at me with apology in your eyes? You were the one hurt. Your face . . . All that happened to me was a little prison time." The first tear slipped out of Joel's eye. It created a clean, jagged line down his dirt-stained face. There were so many different types of scars. "I know how to hate, now," he said. "It's something I learned in prison. I know how to crave revenge, now." He balled his fists, and the muscles in his arms flexed until his veins distended. He looked like a machine. The fear and anger were new to him. They were old to Ava. "The bartender gave us our fortunes that night. None of them were happy."

"Unrequited love. Sad destinies. She was projecting her fears on us," Ava said.

"I am sorry Ava. I am so sorry. I'm sorry for being drunk that night. I'm sorry for not knowing what happened. I'm sorry for being the kind of guy no one thought was worthy of defending. I'm sorry about your accident."

Ava smiled at those words. "It wasn't an accident, Joel. Someone did this to me. Someone did this to you. And both our families. I think we are going to have to trust the police and the media to bring this to the right end."

He shook his head at Ava. "Trust is no longer in my vocabulary."

Ava grabbed his hand. It was warm and rough. She could feel callouses at the place where his fingers met his palm. He returned his face to the sun. Ava looked toward the ground. When she thought to pull her hand away, he gave her hand a squeeze. Why had she needed to see Joel? Trust was no longer in her vocabulary either. Neither was forgiveness, because she still thought of Martin and how she pulled him into the lake.

She needed freedom. She wanted a normal life. She wanted to see her nieces play soccer and eat birthday cake with a dozen girls in tiaras, and make silly blowfish faces into a camera and wear sticky kisses on her face. She wanted her mother to buy her dresses and yet still love her when she wore oversized t-shirts and comfortable shoes. She wanted Nadine to tell people they were twins. She wanted to work at the shelter, no matter the name. She wanted the stares, even from women and children, even if she was afraid. She wanted to show the world she was no longer afraid.

Most of all, she wanted Graham. She wanted to wake up next to him in the morning. She wanted to steal the salty taste from his lips and have no reason to stop. She was always busy saving the world, and he was busy saving his family. Maybe they could share those roles. Maybe they needed to create a new one.

"Maybe trust should be in your vocabulary," Graham said. "People fail us, but we will blame justice or religion or family or any institution but not the specific person responsible for our hurt. Maybe trust is the way to quiet the anger and fear. Maybe the media is going to get the story wrong again, but we will have to trust them or ignore them. We finally know the truth."

Ava let go of Joel's hand and slipped her arms around Graham's waist. Joel didn't seem surprised by the embrace or the kiss Graham placed on her lips.

They turned to leave the field. Eventually, all the weeds would die away and leave behind only the wildflowers.

Epilogue

AVA WANTED TO swim in the ocean. Despite the weeks that had passed, there were still moments when she felt the sediment from Lake Clara Meer coating her body. Sometimes she thought a hand on her ankle pulled her toward unseen water. She believed that there was no limit on the number of times you could die and be reborn. But just as often as she was pulled toward death by a ghostly hand, an angelic one guided her toward the surface.

Sometimes she was reborn in the shower. Sometimes she was reborn in the moonlight. More recently, she was healed in the bright rays of the winter sun.

Graham suggested a trip to Jamaica, the place where he'd been reborn. He booked a quiet villa near the beach, but Ava asked him for something different.

"Either we build houses with your foundation or we go to a noisy resort. Hammering or Bob Marley blaring poolside. I need color and noise."

Graham stepped away from the serving line at Peachtree Missions to make a phone call. It was burrito night. A simple meal in a warm tortilla, and portable if it needed to be. In the distance, a female minister spoke to a small group of women from different backgrounds and religions. The women didn't use a rosary or a prayer mat. They simply held hands. The minister offer a prayer that was simply "Thank you," repeated over and over again. No, "Please God," only a mantra of gratitude.

As Graham walked back to Ava, he paused to pick up a stray napkin on the floor and brought a fresh one for a woman who never let her eyes meet his. When he passed, she glanced up at his retreating form with a smile.

"Done," he said to Ava. He squeezed her hand for a brief moment before returning to his duties. Ava realized that even if he never knew her, he might still spend a winter's night feeding those without. She knew that even without his embrace or his kiss, she loved him.

She went home to pack a simple bag for their trip to the island. She counted the days she slept alone with his voice on the other end of the phone, because he wanted her to be sure about herself and him and his family before he changed their relationship.

She called Joel the night before the trip. The brothers lived in the Donovan hotel as Joel got re-accustomed to life on the outside.

"I'm nervous," she told Joel.

"Ava, I'm not the right person to go to about relationship advice. Why don't you ask your sister?"

"Nadine doesn't wait for anyone or anything. She thinks I'm being silly. The world is as it should be, and I should be making cousins for her kids."

Joel laughed, then he grew somber. "I'm not sure the world will ever be as it should be for us."

Those were exactly the words she was hoping to hear, but she wondered if Graham could love her being partially broken forever.

Joel continued, "But that doesn't mean you can't try to be happy. It also doesn't mean that you should try to be happy with my brother if he isn't the right person for you. You know, set a wild horse free and see if they come back."

"I think this is about me being right for Graham," Ava said. "He is so beautiful. Sometimes it makes me have a new kind of fear. Like I'll lose him."

"You can't lose him if you don't have him," Joel said.

"Promise me you'll call me if you ever need a pep talk," Ava said.

"The day I get a pep talk from you will be a lucky day indeed."

You can't lose him if you don't have him.

The words echoed in her mind as the plane took flight and Graham took her hand. They decided to split the difference between building a house and building sandcastles on the beach. Ava didn't know she could love a place so quickly, but as she exited the airport, the weight of the warm air filled her lungs so completely. She laughed at the sudden heat and humidity.

"It's like you've never breathed before," Graham said.

Ava looked into his eyes and thought it was because of Graham, why she could breathe. And hammer and saw lumber. And take her back to the time of building a tree house for fun with her dad and Nadine. Her mother would draw up the plans and order directions from below.

She was thankful for that memory. She was thankful for Graham at her side to rub her shoulders when the sun went down. There were new friends and food that came from the ground and the trees around them. They stayed in a secluded motel with the team of volunteers. She didn't mind the companion of laughter or the firelight on her face.

They were deep in the mountains. The stars loomed closer in the sky than they did back at home. Beauty was hidden in the trees and the mountains.

"Come here," Graham ordered in their bedroom. He'd been waiting for her kiss. She slid her hand behind his neck. Her hair had been pulled back from her face all day, and she hadn't thought of her scars in weeks. She should tell him she loved him, but he already knew.

"Do you think they'll be mad if we get married before we go back?" she said. "We passed a church and a vicar on our way up here this morning."

"The Anglican church with goats in the graveyard?" he asked. "I noticed it, too, and thought the same thing."

She looked at the ground, smiling and embarrassed. "I just asked you to marry me."

He tilted her head up and kissed her slowly. He pulled his mouth away and smiled. "I just said yes."

Acknowledgments

Writing is my favorite thing in the world. Thank you to my good writing friends Michelle Newcome, Jeanette Cogdell, Marilyn Baron, and LaShon Ison Hill. They have shared tears, heartache, and the occasional hotel room with me. Thanks to Darcy Crowder, Jean Willett, and Marilyn Estes who were with me when I decided to dust off this manuscript one more time. Deepest appreciation to Kristin Leydig Bryant, Craig Bryant, Wendy L. Kinney, Veronica Brown, Edward Ball, Meredith Trotta, Jef Blocker, Rob Gwalteny, and Christina Hodgens for accepting what little I have to give and in return giving me so much.

This book is a result of the knowledge, inspiration, and encouragement of Georgia Romance Writers. Thank you to those who make me hug them: Nancy Knight, Pam Mantovani, Kimberly Brock, Tanya Michaels, Anna Steffl, Sally Kilpatrick, Romily Bernard, and Jennifer McQuiston. Thank you to Romance Writers of America for the gift of a thousand writing friends around world and the amazing experience with the Golden Heart class of 2012, The Firebirds.

I live my life in fiction, but I appreciate Phyllis Aluko and Kirby Clements, Jr. bringing me back to reality with their guidance on legal issues. Thank you to Lila Bradley for her expertise on homelessness and a look inside the Gateway Center. Any errors or omissions are my own.

Itsonlyanovel.com and petitfoursandhottamales.com helped me find my voice. Rachel Haferman helped me get to the finish line. Boot Camp 4 a Cause let me run slowly, but never feel last.

Deborah Smith trusted my words. For that I am forever

humbled and grateful. Thank you Debra Dixon for keeping my secrets. Thank you Bell Bridge Books for accepting me as I am and not making me wear a label.

My family is my breath and my blood. Anything I've achieved is not because I love them, which I do, but because they've loved me. Mom and dad. My sisters and brothers-in-laws. My fearless nieces and nephews. My mother-in-law and my awesome West Coast family. My cat. My kids. My husband. You all are my happily ever after. You are all beautiful.

About Nicki Salcedo

Nicki Salcedo graduated from Stanford University with a degree in English and Creative Writing. She was born in Jamaica and raised in Atlanta, Georgia. She is a member of Romance Writers of America© and a Past President of Georgia Romance Writers. Nicki is a two-time recipient of the Maggie Award of Excellence and a Golden Heart Finalist.

She lives in Atlanta with her four children, husband, and a cat. Nicki thinks everyone should write and loves connecting with readers. For more information go to: www.nickisalcedo.com.

CPSIA information can be obtained at www.ICGtesting.com
Printed in the USA
LVOW11s1423220415

435642LV00006BA/137/P